A BR...
CHIL...
WAITING FOR

BY
MARION LENNOX

MILLS & BOON®
Pure reading pleasure™

First published in Great Britain 2008
Harlequin Mills & Boon Limited,
Eton House, 18-24 Paradise Road, Richmond, Surrey TW9 1SR

© Marion Lennox 2008

ISBN: 978 0 263 86363 5

Set in Times Roman 10½ on 11½ pt
03-1208-51718

Printed and bound in Spain
by Litografia Rosés, S.A., Barcelona

Marion Lennox is a country girl, born on an Australian dairy farm. She moved on—mostly because the cows just weren't interested in her stories! Married to a 'very special doctor', Marion writes Medical™ Romances as well as Mills & Boon® Romances. She used a different name for each category for a while—if you're looking for her past romances, search for author Trisha David as well. She's now had 75 romance novels accepted for publication.

In her non-writing life Marion cares for kids, cats, dogs, chooks and goldfish. She travels, she fights her rampant garden (she's losing) and her house dust (she's lost).

Having spun in circles for the first part of her life, she's now stepped back from her 'other' career, which was teaching statistics at her local university. Finally she's reprioritised her life, figured what's important, and discovered the joys of deep baths, romance and chocolate. Preferably all at the same time!

Recent titles by the same author:

WANTED: ROYAL WIFE AND MOTHER*
HIS ISLAND BRIDE
A ROYAL MARRIAGE OF CONVENIENCE*
THEIR LOST AND FOUND FAMILY†

*In *Mills & Boon® Romance*
†*Crocodile Creek*

CHAPTER ONE

'YOU'LL have to be married or she's going to someone else.'

Tom's words were a bombshell, dropped with devastating effect into the quiet of Charles Wetherby's office. Jill and Charles stared at Lily's uncle in disbelief and mutual shock.

It was Wendy who filled the silence. Wendy was Lily's social worker. She'd handled the details when the little girl's parents had been killed a year ago. There'd been immediate agreement in the aftermath of tragedy. Charles and Jill would care for her.

'Let's just recap, shall we?' Wendy said, buying time in a situation that was threatening to spiral out of control. 'Tom, the situation until now has seemed more than satisfactory.'

It had. Dr Charles Wetherby, medical director of Crocodile Creek Air Sea Rescue Base, was a distant cousin of Lily's mother and a friend of Lily's father. In this remote community relationship meant family. Jill Shaw was the director of nursing at Crocodile Creek, and it had been Jill who Lily had clung to in those first appalling weeks of loss.

'We've loved having her,' Jill whispered.

They had. Neither Jill nor Charles could bear to think of six-year-old Lily with an unknown foster-family. They'd rearranged their living arrangements, knocking a door between their two apartments, becoming partners so Lily could live with them.

They'd become partners in every sense but one, but that one

was what was bothering Tom now. Tom was Lily's legal
guardian. He had six kids by two marriages and he didn't want
his niece, but he'd become increasingly unhappy about her
current living arrangements.

'Charles and Jill have both loved having her,' Wendy reit-
erated, taking in Charles's grim stoicism and Jill's obvious
distress. 'And it's great for Lily to stay in Croc Creek. She was
born here. She's friends with the local kids. Her father's prize
bulls are housed locally and Lily still loves them. Crocodile
Creek provides continuity of identity, and that's imperative.'

But it wasn't an imperative with her uncle.

'The wife's been onto me,' Tom retorted, sounding bellig-
erent. 'People are asking questions. Why don't we take her?
The wife's feeling guilty. Not that we want her, but I'm
damned if I'll keep saying she's fostered. I want her adopted,
and the wife says whoever gets her has to be married. We've
got to be able to say she's gone to a good home.'

Gone to a good home... Like a stray dog, Charles thought
bleakly. Lily wasn't a stray. She was Lily, a chirrupy imp of
a six-year-old who warmed the hearts of everyone around her.

But there were scars. He remembered the crash. The truck had
been a write-off. They'd had to cut the cab open to get to the
bodies of Lily's mother and father, and only then had they discovered the little girl, huddled in a knot of terror behind the seats.

'She needs us,' he said roughly. 'Tom, outwardly Lily's a
bundle of mischief, cheerful and bouncy and into everything.
But she's too self-contained for a kid her age, and almost
every night she has nightmares.'

'We're only just starting to get through to her,' Jill added
urgently, and Charles looked across at his director of nursing
and thought the process was going both ways.

Jill, damaged by a brutal marriage, had escaped to
Crocodile Creek and was only now beginning to relax. Jill was
starting to give her heart to this waif of a little girl.

And Charles...

He'd been a loner for twenty years. It had been no small thing for him to knock a hole in his living-room wall and let Jill and Lily into his life. To give Lily up now…

'We want her,' he said, watching Jill, and he knew by Jill's bleak expression that Jill was expecting the worst.

'Get married, then,' Tom snapped.

'We can't,' Jill whispered.

'Yes, we can,' Charles said, spinning his wheelchair so he was facing Jill directly. 'For Lily's sake…why can't we?'

It seemed they could. When the shock of the question faded, Wendy was beaming her pleasure, seeing in this a really sensible arrangement that meant she didn't have to relocate a child she was still worried about.

Tom was satisfied.

'But do it fast,' he growled. 'I want her off our hands real quick. A month's legal? I'll give you a month to get it done or she's gunna be adopted by someone else.'

He bade them a grim goodbye and departed. No, he didn't want to see Lily before he went. He never did. He might be her uncle but he didn't care.

'This is wonderful,' Wendy said as the door slammed behind him. They were sitting in Charles's office at the Crocodile Creek medical base. The hospital was wide and long and low, opening out to tropical gardens and the sea beyond. Wendy looked out the big French windows to where Lily was swinging on a tyre hanging from a vast Moreton Bay fig tree. 'This is fantastic.'

'It'll mean she can stay here,' Charles said, casting an uneasy glance at Jill.

'It means more than that,' Wendy said warmly. 'What Lily needs is commitment.'

'We are committed,' Jill said, startled out of her silence, but Wendy shook her head.

'No. You're doing the right thing. Neither of you give yourselves. Not really.'

'What the hell do you mean by that?' Charles demanded.

'I mean you two are independent career people. Both of you have been hurt in the past. I'm no mind reader but I can see that. You've gone into your individual shells and you've figured out how not to get hurt. Both of you are lovely people,' she said, gathering her notes with an air of bringing the interview to a close. 'Otherwise I'd never have let Lily stay with you. But both of you need to learn to love. That's what that little girl really needs. Children sense—'

'We do love her,' Jill interrupted hotly.

'Yes, you do,' Wendy said, smiling. 'Enough to marry. It's come as a surprise to me—a joy.' She stooped to kiss Charles on the forehead and then she hugged Jill. Jill stood rigid, unsure.

'You'll figure it out,' Wendy said. 'You and Charles and Lily. It's fantastic. Get yourselves married, learn to expose yourselves to what loving's all about and then I can rip up Lily's case file. Oh, and invite me to the wedding. Tom's not leaving you much time—I guess you'd better start organising bouquets and wedding cake now.'

She left them, skipping down to say goodbye to Lily with a bounce that was astounding for a sixty-year-old, grey-haired social worker.

Jill and Charles were left staring after her.

Not looking at each other.

'What have you done?' Jill said finally into the stillness, and the words sounded almost shocking.

'I guess I've just asked you to marry me,' Charles said.

'I… We can't.'

'Why not?'

'In a month?' she whispered, and he nodded. But he was frowning.

'It's a problem,' he agreed. 'We've got so much on.'

They did. Six months ago a tropical cyclone had ripped a swathe of destruction across the entire coastline of Far North Queensland. The damage had been catastrophic, and only now were things starting to get back to normal. Here on the mainland things were reasonably settled, but their base out at Wallaby Island—a remote clinic plus Charles's pet project, a camp for kids with long-term illnesses or disabilities—had been decimated. With government funding, however, and with the sympathy and enthusiasm of seemingly the entire medical community of Queensland, they had it back together. Better. Bigger. More wonderful. The first kids were arriving this week, and the official opening was on Saturday.

'I guess it doesn't take long to get married,' Charles said cautiously. He wheeled out to the veranda. Jill followed him, unsure what else to do. They stood staring out to sea, lost in their own worlds.

'I shouldn't have said it without asking you,' Charles said at last, and Jill shook her head.

'It doesn't matter.'

'You do want Lily.'

'Of…of course.'

'And this seems the only way.'

'I guess.'

'You *are* divorced?' he asked suddenly, and she bit her lip on a wintry little smile.

'Oh, yes. You think I'd have stayed married…'

'Jill, if you ever want to marry anyone else…' Charles spun his chair again. He was as agile with his chair as many men were on their feet. Shot by accident by his brother when he'd been little more than a kid, Charles had never allowed his body to lose its athletic tone. The damage was between L2 and S1, two of the lowest spinal vertebrae, meaning he had solid upper muscular control. He also had some leg function. He could balance on elbow crutches and move forward, albeit with difficulty. He had little foot control, meaning his feet dragged, and his knees refused to respond, but every day saw him work through an exercise regime that was almost intimidating.

Jill was intimidated. Charles had a powerful intellect and

a commanding presence. Tall, lithe and prematurely grey, with cool grey eyes that twinkled and a personality that was magnetic, he ran the best medical base in Queensland. He might be in a wheelchair, he might be in his forties, but he was one incredibly sexy man.

And he'd asked her to marry him.

No. He'd said they'd marry. There was a difference.

'You don't want to marry me,' she whispered, and he smiled.

'Why would I not? You're a very attractive woman.'

'Yeah, right.'

'No, but you are.'

She stared down at her feet. She and Lily had painted their toenails that morning. Crimson-tipped toes peeped out from beneath faded jeans.

She was wearing ancient jeans and a T-shirt with the sleeves ripped out. She'd pulled her thick chestnut hair back into an elastic band. She left her freckles to fend for themselves. Make-up was for kids.

She was thirty-seven years old. The young medics who worked in Crocodile Creek hospital looked fabulous, young, glowing, eager. In comparison Jill felt old. Worn out with life.

'You know you can trust me in a marriage,' Charles said gently. 'It's in name only. If you hate the idea…'

She turned to face him. Charles. Wise, intelligent, astringent. Funny, sad, intensely private.

How could she think of marrying him?

'O-of course it w-would be in name only,' she stammered. 'I… You know I wouldn't…'

'I know you wouldn't,' he said, sounding suddenly tired.

'Tom won't let Lily stay with us if we don't marry,' she said, turning away from him. Fighting for composure. 'And…and you do want Lily?'

'You want Lily, too,' he said. 'Don't you?'

She stared out across the garden at Lily, swinging higher and higher. Did she want a daughter?

More than anything else in the world, she thought. Until Lily's parents had died her life had been…a void.

Her life had been a void since she'd walked out on her marriage. Or maybe it had been a void since she'd married.

'What the hell did he do to you to make you so fearful?' Charles demanded suddenly, and Jill shook her head.

'I'm not fearful.'

'Not in your work, you're not. Put bluntly, you're the best nurse it's ever been my privilege to work with. But in your private life…'

'I'm fine.'

'You've kept yourself to yourself ever since you've been here.'

'And you've kept yourself to yourself for even longer.'

'Maybe I have more reason,' he muttered. 'Hell, Jill, do you think we can make a marriage work?'

'I… How different would it be from what it is now?'

'I guess not much,' he conceded. 'I'd need to buy you a ring.'

'You don't.'

'No, that much I do,' he said. 'Let's make this official straight away.' He glanced at his watch. 'But things are tight. We've got Muriel Mooronwa's hernia operation in half an hour, and I've promised to assist Cal. If things are straightforward we might catch the shops before closing.' He grimaced. 'And the paperwork…that'll take time and I need to go to the island tomorrow.' He frowned, thinking it through. 'You know I've told Lily I'll take her with me. Why not rearrange the roster and come with us? We could sort out the details over there.'

'I can't,' she said flatly. 'Someone senior has to stay here.'

'I can ask Gina and Cal to stay. Cal's so much second in command here now he's practically in charge.'

'He's not a nurse. Doctors think they know everything but when it comes to practicalities they're useless.'

'You don't want—'

'No,' she said flatly, and would have stepped away but Charles's hand came out and caught her wrist. Urgent.

'Jill, this doesn't have to happen. I'm not marrying you against your will.'

'Of course not,' she said dully, and a flash of anger crossed Charles's face.

'You'll have to do better than that,' he snapped. 'I want no submissive wife.'

'What's that supposed to mean?'

'It means I employ you as a director of nursing and I get a competent, bossy, sometimes funny, sometimes emotionally involved woman who keeps my nursing staff happy. It's that woman I'm asking to marry me—not the echo of what you once had with Kelvin.'

'I'm over Kelvin.'

'You're not,' he said gently. 'I know you're not. I'd like to murder the bottom-feeding low-life. More than anything else, Jill, I'd like to wipe the slate clean so you can start afresh. Find some great guy who can give you a normal life—kids, dancing, loving, the whole box and dice. But I can't. OK, I can't have them either. We're stuck with what life's thrown at us. But between us we want to give Lily a great home. She makes us both smile, we make her smile, and that counts for everything. It's a start, Jill. A need to make a kid smile. Is it a basis for a marriage?'

She took a deep breath. She turned and leaned back on the veranda rail so she was looking down at him.

'I sound appallingly ungrateful,' she whispered.

'You don't. You sound as confused as I am.'

'You're burying your dreams.'

'I don't do dreams,' he said roughly. 'We've both been there, Jill. We both know that life slaps you round if you don't keep a head on your shoulders. But what we have... Friendship. Respect. Lily. Is it enough to build a marriage?'

'For Lily's sake?'

'Not completely,' he said, and he looked out to where Lily was swinging so high she just about swung over the branch. 'Just a little bit for our sakes.'

'Because we love Lily,' Jill whispered.

'And because the arrangement suits us.'

'I guess we already have a ruddy great hole in our living-room wall.'

'We may as well make it permanent,' Charles said. He'd released her hand. He put his hands on the arms of his wheel-chair as if he meant to push himself to his feet, but Jill took a step away and he obviously thought better of it. 'What do you say, Jill? For all our sakes…will you marry me?'

'As long…as long as you don't expect a real marriage.'

'Outwardly at least it has to be real. Lily needs to know that we're marrying and we're her adoptive parents.'

'She calls us Jill and Charles,' Jill said inconsequentially.

'Wendy says that's OK.'

'Yes, but I'd really like her to call me…' She faltered. 'But I guess that's something I can get over. Charles, if you really mean it…'

'I really mean it.'

'Then I'll marry you,' she whispered, and despite the enormity of their decision Charles's eyes creased into laughter.

'I'm supposed to get down on bended knee.'

'And I'm supposed to blush and simper.'

'I guess we make do with what we've got.' He caught her hand again and before she guessed what he intended he lifted and lightly brushed the back of her hand with a kiss. 'It makes sense, Jill. There's no one I'd rather marry.'

The sound of laughter echoed from the pathway. Across the lawn was the doctors' house, a residence filled with young doctors from around the world. Doctors came here and gave a year or two's service to the remote medical base.

Two young women were coming along the path now, in white coats, stethoscopes around their necks.

They were young and carefree and gorgeous.

There was no one Charles would rather marry? Jill doubted that. He was gorgeous, she thought. His disability was nothing.

But it wasn't nothing in his eyes. It would always stop him giving his heart.

If he couldn't give his heart, she may as well marry him, she thought. And, hey…

A tiny part of her…just a tiny part…thought marriage to Charles Wetherby might be…well…interesting?

Quite simply, Charles was the sexiest man ever to be stuck in a wheelchair, voted so by every single female medic who ever came here.

'OK,' she said, and managed a smile. The smile even felt right.

'OK, what?'

'I'll marry you.'

'Fine,' he said, and grinned and let her hand go. 'Let's get this hernia organised and go into town and find us a ring.'

'A ring…'

'A ruddy great diamond,' he said. 'If we're doing this at all, we're doing it properly.'

'Charles, no.'

'Jill, yes,' he said, and spun his wheelchair to the end of the veranda where the ramp gave him access to the outside path. Decision made. Time to move on.

'Let's tell Lily,' he said. 'She needs to approve. But, hell, we only have a month to make this legal. We may as well stop wasting time.'

'Don't…don't tell Lily yet.' It seemed too fast. Too sudden.

'Tonight, then, when we tuck her into bed,' Charles said. 'But it has to be done. Let's get a move on.'

CHAPTER TWO

HE NEVER wasted time. Charles Wetherby didn't know what it was to stand still.

Jill stood beside Cal and handed over instruments as Cal carefully repaired Muriel Mooronwa's inguinal hernia. It should have been repaired months ago. It had been seriously interfering with her life for over a year, but that Muriel agreed to have the operation at all was a huge achievement.

It was down to Charles, Jill thought. Ten years ago women like Muriel would have become more and more incapacitated, and probably ended up dying needlessly as the hernia strangulated. Muriel, like so many of the population round Crocodile Creek, was an indigenous Australian who'd been raised in a tribal community. She distrusted cities and all they represented. She distrusted white doctors. But Charles had brought these people a medical service second to none.

From the time Charles had been shot, his wealthy farming family had deemed him useless. Their loss had been the greater gain of this entire region. Charles had gone to medical school with a mission, to return here and set up a service other remote communities could only dream of. He'd had the vision to set up a doctors' residence which attracted medics from all over the world. He talked doctors such as Cal, a top-flight surgeon, and Gina, an American cardiologist, into staying long term. His enthusiasm was infectious. Wherever you went, people were caught up in Charles's projects.

Like Wallaby Island's kids' camp. As soon as his remote air sea rescue service was established Charles had got bored, looking for something else to do. The camp for disabled kids, bringing kids from all over Australia for the holiday of a lifetime, was brilliant in its intent. It brought kids to the tropics to have fun and it provided first-class rehabilitation facilities while that happened.

He acted on impulse, Jill thought as she worked beside him. What sort of impulse had had him asking her to marry him?

'You're daydreaming,' Charles said softly. The main part of the procedure was over now. Cal was stitching, making sure the job was perfect. There was time for his helpers to stand back. Or, in Charles's case, to wheel back. He had a special stool he used in theatre. He'd devised it himself so he could be on a level with what was going on and swivel and move at need. As director of the entire base it was reasonable to assume he didn't need to act in a hands-on capacity, but the day Charles stopped working...

It'd kill him, Jill thought. The man was driven.

'You're dreaming diamonds?' Charles said, teasing, and Jill gasped.

'What...? No!'

'Diamonds,' Cal said, eyes widening. 'Diamonds!'

'Maybe just one diamond,' Charles said. 'Jill, seeing Gina and Cal are our babysitters-in-chief, I figure maybe Cal should be the first to know.'

'You guys are getting married?' Cal said incredulously.

'Only because of Lily,' Jill said in a rush, and the pleasure in Cal's eyes faded a little.

'Why?'

'If we don't get married Lily gets adopted by someone else,' Charles said. 'We're sort of used to her being around.'

'You mean you love her,' Cal said gently, and the smile returned. 'You want to tell me how it happened?'

'Her uncle wants her adopted,' Charles explained. 'He's her legal guardian. He wants a married couple.' He turned to the tray of surgical instruments and focused on what needed attention.

Nothing needed attention.

'We can't let her go,' Jill said warmly, life returning to her voice. 'We all love her.'

'Of course we do,' Cal said. Lily was playing with Gina and Cal's small son, CJ, right now. CJ and Lily were best friends. They were in and out of each other's houses, they slept over at each other's places; in fact, sometimes Charles thought Lily regarded Gina and Cal as just as much her parents as he and Jill.

It was a problem, he thought. Oh, it made life easy that Lily transferred her affections to whoever she was with, but Wendy worried that the child's superficial attachments were the result of trauma.

It didn't matter, Charles thought. It'd settle.

'So when's the date?' Cal asked, and Charles looked questioningly at Jill.

'I... We need to do it within a month.'

'Hey, it's a magnificent excuse for a party. It'll be headline news...'

'Private ceremony,' Charles said before he thought about it. 'No fuss.'

'No fuss,' Jill agreed, and Charles looked sharply up at her. Kicking himself. He'd done it again. He'd made the decision without consulting her.

'And no photographs,' she said. Her voice was flat, inflexionless. No joy there.

Of course not. She'd had the marriage from hell the first time round. Marriage could never be something she approached with joy.

He knew few details of her past, and those he hadn't gained from Jill. His friend Harry, the Crocodile Creek policeman, had passed on information to Charles when he'd become involved with Jill that he'd thought might be important.

Married absurdly young and with no family support, Harry reported that Jill's marriage had been a nightmare of abuse. She'd tried to run, but she'd been hauled back, time and time again. Her final attempt to defy her husband had nearly cost her life. Only the fact that there'd been a couple of tourists on the jetty as Jill had staggered from her husband's fishing boat had saved her life.

But despite her appalling marriage, Jill Shaw was a woman of intelligence and courage. She'd still been young enough to start a new life. Cautiously, and with the encouragement from women she met at the refuge she'd ended up in after she'd been discharged from hospital, she'd applied for a nursing course as far away from the scene of her marriage as she'd been able to. She still feared Kelvin and had changed her name to keep hidden, but she'd moved on. She'd lived on the smell of an oily rag to get what she wanted.

She'd graduated with honours, she'd embraced her profession and when she'd applied to Crocodile Creek—it had to be one of the most remote nursing jobs in Australia—Charles hadn't believed his luck.

But she wasn't happy. Normally bossy and acerbic, with a wry sense of humour, the events of the afternoon seemed to have winded her. Was she afraid? Of more than her ex-husband finding her? Hell, she had to know he'd never hurt her. And she'd agreed. She did love Lily, he thought. She wanted this.

He was going to Wallaby Island tomorrow without her. He had to have her smile about this—he had to have her feeling sure before he went.

'Cal, we're finished now,' he said, maybe more roughly than he intended. 'Do you think you and Gina can hang on to Lily for a few more hours?'

'Of course,' Cal said easily. 'We're packing to go to

Wallaby Island tomorrow. Having Lily will get CJ out of our hair while we organise ourselves.'

'Fine,' Charles said. He had his own packing to do but it'd have to wait. 'Don't mention what's happening to Lily—we want to tell her ourselves tonight. But Jill and I are going out to dinner and we need to leave now.'

'It's only four now,' Jill said, startled. 'What's the rush?'

'We need to get changed,' Charles said. 'And we need to get into town before the jeweller shuts. I've never been engaged before and if we're going to do this…Jill, let's do this in style.'

He wouldn't listen to her objections. She didn't need a ring. She didn't need…marriage.

What was she doing?

Jill stood in her bare little bedroom and gazed into her wardrobe with a sense of helplessness. She was going out to dinner with Charles. She should wear clean jeans and a neat white shirt.

'A dress,' Charles called from his bedroom, and she winced.

A dress. The outfit she'd bought for the weddings?

It was an occupational hazard, working in Crocodile Creek, she thought ruefully. So many young medics came here to work that romance was inevitable. They'd had, what, eight weddings in the last year? So much so that the locals laughingly referred to the doctors' house as the Wedding Chapel.

She'd never lived in the doctors' house. She valued her independence too much.

What was she doing?

She wanted Lily. It was like an ache. From the time she'd held her, the night her parents had been killed, her heart had gone out to the little girl. Even Lily's fierce independence, the way she held herself just slightly aloof from affection… Jill could understand it and respect it.

'Dress?' Charles called again, and she smiled. He was as

bossy as she was. But not…autocratic. Never violent. She'd seen him in some pretty stressful situations. There'd been a family feud. His brother had been responsible for his injury, yet his father had vented his fury on Charles. He'd considered his injured son useless.

Charles had never railed against the unfairness of fate. He'd taken his share of a vast inheritance—a share which his father hadn't legally been able to keep from him—and he'd proceeded to set up this medical base. He'd funnelled his anger and his frustration into good.

He deserved…

A dress.

OK. She tugged her only dress from its hanger—a creamy silk sliver of a frock that hugged her figure, that draped in a cowl collar low around her breasts, no sleeves, a classy garment Gina had bullied her into for Kate and Hamish's wedding. She slipped it on, and then tugged her hair from its customary elastic band.

Her glossy chestnut curls had once been a source of pride. She brushed them now. They fell to her shoulders. She looked younger this way, she thought as she stared into the mirror. There was no grey in her hair yet.

She was a woman about to choose her engagement ring…

It was nonsense. She shoved her feet into sandals, grabbed her purse and headed for the door.

And stopped and returned to the mirror.

She stared at her reflection for a long moment, then sighed and grabbed a compact and swiped powder over her freckles. She put on lipstick that had been used, what, eight times for eight weddings?

Hers would be the ninth?

'It's nonsense,' she whispered, but as she put the lid back on her lipstick she caught sight of her reflection and paused.

'Not too bad for thirty-seven,' she whispered. 'And you're going to marry Charles.'

It was a sensible option. But…Charles.

She couldn't quite suppress a quiver of excitement. He really was…

'Just Charles,' she said to herself firmly. 'Medical director of Croc Creek. Your boss.

'Your husband?

'Get real,' she told her reflection. She stuck her tongue out at herself, grinned and went to meet her fiancé.

He liked it. She emerged from her bedroom and Charles was waiting. His eyes crinkled in the way she loved.

'Hey,' he said softly. 'What's the occasion? An engagement or something?'

Charles had made an effort, too. He was wearing casual cream trousers and a soft, cream, open-necked shirt. Quality stuff. Clothes that made him look even sexier than he usually did.

He hadn't lost muscle mass, as many paraplegics did, Jill thought. His injury could almost be classified as cauda equina rather than complete paraplegia—a damage to the nerves at the base of his spine. He pushed himself, standing every day, forcing his legs to retain some strength. It'd be much easier to stay in the wheelchair but that had never been Charles's way—taking the easy option.

He was great, she thought. The most fantastic boss…

But a husband?

'Lily's OK?' she asked.

'Settled at Cal and Gina's.'

Her face clouded. 'You know, I wish—'

'That she wasn't quite as happy to go to strangers,' he said softly. 'I know. It's what Wendy says. Tom's right in a way. She needs permanence. Even commitment. That's what we're doing now. Let's go buy us an engagement ring.'

The jeweller was obsequious, eager and shocked. He tried to usher them into the door, tugging Charles's wheelchair sideways in an unnecessary effort to help, and came close to upending him in the process. By the time Charles extricated himself from his unwelcome aid, the man had realised the potential of his customers.

'Well,' he said as he tugged out trays of his biggest diamonds. 'Never did I think I'd have the pleasure of selling an engagement ring to the medical director of Crocodile Creek. And you a Wetherby. I sold an engagement ring to your brother. He runs the farm now, doesn't he? Such a shame about your accident. Not that you haven't done very well for yourself. A healthy man could hardly have done more. You're still a Wetherby, though, sir. Now, your brother purchased a one and a half carat diamond when he got engaged. If you'd warned me… I don't have anything near that quality at the moment, but if you'd like to choose a style, I can have a selection flown in tomorrow. As big as you like,' he said expansively. 'You're a lucky lady, miss.'

'Yes,' Jill said woodenly. The way the jeweller looked at Charles was patronising, she thought. She'd spent enough time with Charles to pick up on the way people talked to him. This guy was doing it wrong. He was talking to Charles but keeping eye contact with her. He was making her know he was being kind to the guy in the wheelchair. And the way Charles had looked when he'd mentioned his brother…

She hated this shop. She hated these ostentatious diamonds. How big was the man saying this diamond should be?

Would Charles like her to have a bigger diamond than his brother's wife?

'What would you like, Jill?' Charles asked gently, and she shook herself out of her anger and tried to make a choice. She had to do this.

'Any diamond's fine,' she said. 'I guess….however big you want.'

'However big *I* want?'

He was quizzing her. He had this ability to figure what she

thought almost before she thought it herself. The ability scared her.

Maybe Charles scared her.

'You don't really want a diamond, do you?' he said.

'If you think—'

'I don't think,' he said with another flash of irritation. 'It's you who gets to wear the thing. Some of these rings are really….'

'Ostentatious?' she said before she could help herself, and Charles's face relaxed. He smiled wryly, though the touch of anger remained.

'I'm right, aren't I? You hate these as much as I do.'

'I suspect we do need an engagement ring, though,' she said. 'If you're planning on telling everyone we're engaged.'

'I *am* planning on telling everyone we're engaged.' He hesitated and then held out his hand to the jeweller. 'Sorry, Alf,' he said bluntly. 'I've a lady with simple tastes. I'm thinking it's one of the reasons I've asked her to marry me, so we'll not go against that. Thank you for your help and good day. Coming, Jill?'

'We're not…?'

'No, we're not,' he said forcefully, and propelled his chair out the door before she could argue.

By the time Jill caught him up he was half a block away. She had to run to catch up.

He realised, slowed and spun to face her.

'Sorry,' he said, rueful. 'Telling me the size of my brother's engagement ring pushed a few buttons I don't like to have pushed.'

'I can see that,' she said cautiously. 'And the way he treated you…'

'I don't care about the way he treated me. I'm used to it. But you… You don't really want a three-carat diamond ring?'

'I don't want any ring.' She hesitated, looking down at her hands. They were work hands, scrubbed a hundred times a day in her job as a nurse. They were red and a bit wrinkled. The nails were as short as she could cut them.

'I'd look ridiculous with a diamond.'

'How about an opal?' Charles asked, and she hesitated. 'If you don't want one, just say so.'

'I love opals,' she said cautiously. 'But—'

'But nothing. George Meredith's in town. Have you met him? He's a local prospector—he spends his time scraping in dirt anywhere from here to Longreach. What he doesn't know about opals isn't worth knowing. I know he's in town because I saw him for a dodgy back this morning. I told him no digging for a week, to stay in town, get himself a decent bed and put his feet up. He'll be down at the hotel. I also know he has some really decent rock. Let's go and take a look.'

He had more than decent rock. He had ready-made jewellery.

'I don't normally make it up,' he told them. A big, shy man, quietly spoken but with enormous pride in the stones he produced to show them, he stood back as they fingered his fabulous collection. 'I sell it on to dealers. But a mate of mine's done some half-decent work and while the back's been bad he's been teaching me to do a bit. These are the ones I'm happiest with. When me back's a bit better I'm heading to Cairns—I reckon the big tourist places will snap this lot up. Hang on a sec.'

They hung on. George had spread his stones out on the coverlet of his hotel bed for them to see. Now he delved into a battered suitcase and produced a can of aftershave. He glanced suspiciously at his visitors, then grinned as if he'd decided suspicions here were ridiculous, but all the same he turned his back on them so they couldn't see what he was doing. He twiddled for a bit and then spun back to face them. The aftershave can was open at the base and a small, chamois pouch was lying in his open palm.

He opened it with care, unwrapping individual packages. Laying their contents on a pillow.

Four rings and two pendants. Each one made Jill gasp.

'They're black opal,' George said with satisfaction. 'You won't find better stuff than this anywhere in the world. You like them?'

Did she like them? Jill stared down at the cluster of small opals and thought she'd never seen anything lovelier.

She lifted one, drawn to it before all the others. It was the smallest stone, a rough-shaped opal set in a gold ring. The stone was deep, turquoise green, with black in its depths. But there was fire, tiny slivers of red that looked like fissures in the rock, exposing flames deep down. The opal looked as if it had been set in the gold in the ground, wedged there for centuries, washed by oceans, weathered to the thing of beauty it was now.

She'd never seen anything so beautiful.

'Put it on,' George prodded, and as she didn't move Charles lifted it from her, took her ring finger and slid the ring home.

It might have been made for her.

She gazed down at it and blinked. And tried to think of something to say. And blinked again.

'I think we have a sale,' Charles said in satisfaction. Both men were smiling at her now, like two avuncular genies.

'It ought to go on a hand like that,' George said. 'You know, that stone… I almost decided to keep it. I couldn't bear to think of it on some fancy woman's hand, sitting among half a dozen diamonds and sapphires and the like. If you don't mind me saying so, ma'am,' he said, 'your hands are right for it. Worn a bit. Ready for something as lovely.'

'Not a bad pitch,' Charles said appreciatively.

'I mean it,' George growled, and from the depth of emotion in his voice Jill knew he did.

But…

'I can't,' she whispered. 'This is black opal.' She hadn't lived in a place such as Crocodile Creek without knowing the value of such a stone. 'You can't…'

'I can,' Charles said solidly. 'Jill, why don't you go down to the bar while George and I talk business?'

'I—'

'Go,' he said, and propelled her firmly out the door.

They went to dinner at the Athina. They were greeted with pleasure and hugs and exclamations of delight before they so much as made it to their table.

Word was all over town.

'Oh, but it's beautiful,' Sophia Poulos said mistily, looking at the ring and sighing her happiness. 'If you two knew how much we hoped this would happen…'

'We're only doing this for Lily,' Jill said, startled, but Sophia beamed some more.

'Nonsense. You wear a beautiful ring. You wear a beautiful dress. You are a beautiful woman and Dr Wetherby…he's a very handsome man, eh? And don't tell me you haven't noticed. You're doing this for Lily? In my eye!' She gave a snort of derision and headed back to her kitchen. 'Hey,' she yelled to her husband. 'We have lovers on table one. Champagne on the house.'

It was silly. It was embarrassing. It was also kind of fun. But as the meal wore on, as the attention of the restaurant patrons turned away, there was a sudden silence. It stretched out a little too long.

It's just Charles, Jill told herself, feeling absurdly self-conscious. It's just my boss.

'What's happening tomorrow?' she asked, and it was the right thing to ask for it slid things back into a work perspective. Here they were comfortable. For the last eight years they'd worked side by side to make their medical service the best.

'There's three days' work happening tomorrow,' Charles growled. In the project ahead Charles held passion. The kids' camp on Wallaby Island had been a dream of Charles's since he'd returned to Crocodile Creek. Jill had been caught up in his enthusiasm and had been as devastated as Charles when the cyclone had wreaked such havoc.

But tragedy could turn to good. With public attention and sympathy focussed on the region, funding had been forthcoming to turn the place into a facility beyond their imagination. Charles was heading there tomorrow to welcome the first kids to the restored and extended camp. It was a wonder he'd found time to talk to the social worker about Lily, Jill thought ruefully, much less take this evening off to wine and dine a fiancée.

And give her a ring.

As they talked about their plans—or, rather, Charles talked and Jill listened—her eyes kept drifting to her ring.

She'd never owned anything so beautiful. Despite what George said, it didn't look right on her work-worn hand.

But Charles had always known what she was thinking. She had to learn to factor that in. 'It's perfect,' he said gently, interrupting what he was saying to reassure her, and she flushed.

'I'm sorry. I didn't mean…'

'It's me who should be sorry. This is no night to be talking about work.'

'We don't have a lot more in common,' she said bluntly, and then bit her lip. She hadn't meant to sound so…tart.

Maybe she was tart. Maybe that was how she always sounded. She'd stop pretences years ago.

One of the reasons she'd relaxed with Charles over the years had been that he seemed to appreciate blunt talking. He asked for her opinion and he got it.

She needed to soften, though, she thought. He wouldn't want a wife who shot her mouth off.

'We have Lily in common,' he reminded her, and she nodded.

Of course. But… 'I'm not sure why you want her,' she said cautiously. 'I know your reaction when her parents died was the same as mine—overwhelming sadness. But you do already have a daughter.'

'I have Kate,' he said. 'A twenty-seven-year-old daughter I've only known for the last few months.'

'You must have loved her mother.'

'We all did,' he said ruefully. 'Maryanne was gorgeous. She was wild and loving and did what she pleased. I wasn't the only one in love with her. You know that's what caused the rift in my family? Philip, my brother, shot me by accident, but he put the blame on a mate of mine who also loved Maryanne. The repercussions of that can still be felt today. Anyway, that's what happened. I was injured and was sent to the city. Apparently Maryanne was in the early stages of pregnancy but didn't tell anyone. Certainly not me. A rushed marriage to a young man who was little more than a boy, and who was facing a life of paraplegia…that would never be Maryanne's style.

'By the time I was well enough to return here she'd disappeared down south. Apparently she had Kate adopted and then proceeded to have a very good life. The first I knew of it was when Kate arrived on the scene just before the cyclone.'

He said it lightly. He said it almost as if it didn't hurt, but there was enough in those few words to let Jill see underneath. A young man wildly in love, deserted seemingly because of his paraplegia. Knowing later he'd fathered a child, but Maryanne had not deemed it worth telling him. It was more of the same, she thought. More of the treatment meted out by the jeweller.

Charles as a young man would have been gorgeous. She knew enough of his family background to know he was also rich. Maryanne might well have chosen another course altogether if she hadn't classified the father of her child as something…

Well, it was all conjecture, Jill thought harshly. Charles must have done his own agonising. It wasn't for her to do his agonising for him.

'But it does mean you have a daughter,' she said gently into the silence.

'I do,' he said. 'But I missed out on the whole damned lot.

With Lily it's a bit like being given the chance again.' He hesitated. 'OK. Enough. What about you?'

'Me?' she said, startled.

'All I know of your background is from other people,' he said. 'Maybe if we're to be married I ought to know a bit more.'

'You don't want to know about Kelvin.'

'Harry told me he was in jail.'

'He had a five-year sentence for…for hurting me. I'm still…'

'Afraid of him?'

'He used to say he'd kill me if I left him,' she whispered. 'He demonstrated it enough for me to believe him.'

'You think he's still a threat?'

'He doesn't know I'm here. You know that. You know I've changed my name. Judy Standford, dumb, bashed wife of a fisherman down south, to Jill Shaw, director of nursing at Croc Creek. But he'll still be looking.'

'Surely after so many years…'

'What Kelvin owns he'll believe he owns to the end,' she said bleakly. 'He'd want me dead rather than see me free.'

'Why the hell did you marry him?' he asked savagely.

'The oldest reason in the world,' she said. 'Like you and Maryanne, only maybe without the passion. I was sixteen. A kid. Kelvin was a biker, a mate of my oldest brother, Rick. Rick agreed I could go with them to a music festival. I was way out of my depth and I ended up pregnant. My dad…well, my dad was as violent in his way as Kelvin. Kelvin agreed to marry me and I was terrified enough to do it. Only then I lost the baby. And when I tried to leave… It just…' She stopped, seeming too distressed to go on.

'You don't have to explain to me,' Charles said gently. 'But, even after you left, you never thought you'd marry again? You never thought you'd like a child?'

'Of course I'd like a child,' she said explosively. 'I was seven months pregnant when I lost my little girl. I hadn't realised…until I held Lily…'

'So Lily's a second chance for both of us.' He reached over the table and took her ring hand, folding it between both of his. The warmth and strength of his hold gave her pause.

She'd been close to tears. Close to fury. His hold grounded her, settled her. Made her feel she had roots. But it also left her feeling out of her depth.

'D-don't,' she said, and tugged back.

'We need to show a bit of affection,' Charles said wryly. 'If we're to pull off a marriage that doesn't look like a sham.'

'It doesn't matter if it is a sham.'

'You see, I'm thinking that's where you might be wrong,' he said. 'We've been given Lily. It's a huge gift.'

'We should be home with her now.'

'She doesn't need us now,' Charles said. 'That's the problem. Oh, she needs us in that we're providing security whether she knows it or not. But if we said she was to live with Gina and Cal…'

'She'd be upset,' Jill said. She tugged her hand away and stared down into the depths of her ring. 'Or she'd be more upset,' she amended. 'She's traumatised.'

'She won't let the psychologists near.' Charles sighed. 'Well, you know the problems as well as I do. Do we tell her tonight that we're getting married? That she can stay with us for ever?'

'Cal knows. Gina knows. Sophia Poulos knows. We'd better do it or she'll be the last in Croc Creek to find out.'

CHAPTER THREE

CHARLES settled the bill and they went out into the balmy night. On another occasion they might have walked here—or wheeled here, Jill corrected herself. Charles never let being in a chair stop him going places. The strength in his arms was colossal and he could push his chair long after those around him were tired from walking.

But there was packing to do tonight and they needed to collect Lily before it got too late. So they'd driven. Or Charles had driven. He was almost as fast getting into the car as a normal driver, opening the door, sliding into the driver seat, clipping his chair closed and swinging it into the rear seat behind him. By the time Jill had adjusted the drapes of her dress they were already moving out onto the road.

He was a normal guy, Jill thought as she tried to focus on the road ahead, and she swallowed. A normal husband. Did he realise what that did to her?

It terrified her.

She'd agreed to this marriage why? Because she loved Lily. Because she couldn't bear that Lily be further dislocated.

Because Charles was in a wheelchair and would make no demands on her as a wife?

Maybe that had been a factor, she conceded. Up until now Charles's paraplegia had made this marriage seem…safer? A sexless marriage.

But maybe that was dumb. His injury was so low that maybe…maybe…

Maybe nothing. It didn't matter, either way. She trusted Charles. It'd be OK.

But she glanced sideways at his profile in the moonlight. The lean, angular features of a strongly boned face. The crinkles around his eyes where years of laughter had left their mark. And pain. He'd never admit it but you didn't suffer the type of injury he'd endured without pain.

She loved the way his hair crinkled at the roots and then became wavy—just a little. She loved the silver in it. Premature grey was so damned sexy in a male…

Sexy. See, there was the thing. Charles didn't see himself as sexy so neither should she. She was right to think of his paraplegia as her security. She had to keep thinking of him as disabled, because if she kept thinking of him as sexy this marriage of convenience would never work. She ought to run rather than risk it.

But she was tired of running. She wanted a home. A home, a husband, a daughter.

Charles.

If Kelvin found out, he'd kill them all.

Was she being paranoid? The logical part of her said yes. The part of her that had been controlled by Kelvin said she wasn't being paranoid at all.

'What are you thinking?' he asked, his voice a little strained. Maybe he was finding this as hard as she was.

'That maybe it's good for you that you're going to Wallaby Island tomorrow,' she said, and for the life of her she couldn't stop her voice from sounding faintly waspish. 'This place is going to be awash with gossip, and you and Lily will have escaped.'

'Just snap their noses off when they ask to see your ring,' he said. 'That'll sort them out.'

'You think I'm…prickly.'

'I *know* you're prickly.'

'Charles, why do you want to marry me?' she burst out. 'I'm plain and I'm bossy and I'm old.'

'Now, that,' Charles said solemnly, 'is ridiculous.'

'Is it?'

'So why do you want to marry me?' he demanded. 'I'm in a wheelchair.'

'That's just as ridiculous.'

'You don't think you want to marry me *because* I'm in a wheelchair?'

'Because I feel sorry for you?' she muttered. 'Fat chance.'

'You don't feel sorry for me?'

'Anyone feeling sorry for you gets their heads bitten off.'

'So you're scared of me.'

'I'm not,' she said, and then decided to be honest. 'Or not very much.'

'So let me get this straight,' he said slowly. 'You're thinking you're plain and bossy and old, you're scared of me but you've decided to marry me anyway.'

'It does sound dumb,' she admitted.

'Yeah,' he agreed. 'With all the romance in the air around Croc Creek, the place practically sizzles.'

'It's just as well it doesn't sizzle near us, then.'

'Not even a bit?'

'Of course not. I mean, look at us. We've discussed this sensibly. We've bought an engagement ring. We haven't even kissed.'

'I kissed your hand.'

'You did,' she said. 'Um…yeah. Very nice it was, too.'

'You want to be kissed?'

'No!'

'We ought to,' he said thoughtfully. 'I mean…we do intend to make a marriage out of it. We could just try.'

'Charles, don't.'

'Because you're plain and old and bossy?'

'No, because…'

'Because I'm in a wheelchair?'

'No!'

'Then why?' he demanded, and there was suddenly frustration in his voice. 'Why the hell not?'

'Because we don't…'

'Deserve it?' He glanced over at her. She was staring straight into the night, trying to figure out what to say. What to do. She was fingering her engagement ring like it was burning.

'Jill, don't look like that.'

'Like what?'

'Hell,' he said again, and before she knew what he intended he'd steered the car onto the verge. They were at the foot of the bridge beside Crocodile Creek. There was a sloping sandbank running down to the water.

In other circumstances a romantic couple might get out and wander down to the water's edge to admire the moonbeams glimmering over the water's dark surface.

Yeah, in other circumstances a couple might get taken by a crocodile. Getting out here was for fools.

Stopping here was for fools.

'Jill, I'm not marrying any woman who's afraid of me,' Charles said steadily into the darkness.

'I'm not…'

'Look at me and say it.'

She turned and looked at him. He gazed steadily back, serious, questioning.

She knew this man. She'd worked with him for years. He was the best doctor in Crocodile Creek.

He loved Lily. He was doing this to give her a daughter.

'I'm not afraid of you,' she said, and it was true. She trusted him. She knew it at every logical level. It was only the thought of marriage that had her terrified.

But this was Charles. Charles!

'It'll be OK,' Charles said softly, and he caught her hands

and tugged her toward him. 'Jill, I don't think you're plain or bossy or old.' Then he smiled, that crinkly, crooked smile that transformed his face. The smile she loved. 'OK, maybe bossy,' he conceded. 'But bossy's good for a director of nursing. Maybe bossy's even good for a mum, and that's what you're going to be. It'll be fine. It might even be fantastic. Let's give it our best shot, eh?'

And he tugged her close—and he kissed her.

She hadn't been kissed for how long?

Years and years and years. Her kissing skills had lain dormant, forgotten. Buried.

But not dead.

She'd last kissed with passion when she'd been a teenager. She'd forgotten…or she'd never known…

Strong, warm hands holding her face, centring her so he could find her mouth. Lips meeting lips. Warmth meeting warmth.

Not warmth. Fire.

That was what it felt like. A rush of heat so intense that it sent shock waves jolting through her body. She felt her lips open, she felt his mouth merge with hers…

It was like moving into another dimension.

Her hands lifted involuntarily, her fingers raking his hair, firming their link. Not that there was a need for such firming. She couldn't back away from this.

This magic.

It was a feeling so intense it seemed she was almost out of her body. Transformed into something she'd never been, or if she had she'd long forgotten. A girl, a woman who could melt with pure desire.

For just a moment she let herself fall. She let herself be swept away, feeling how she could feel if she were a girl again and life was before her and she didn't know what happened to women who surrendered control.

Kelvin had called her an ugly cow—over and over until she'd believed it totally. But maybe…just maybe he was wrong.

This was delicious, delectable, dangerous… Seductive in its sweetness. Overwhelming in its demands. For he wasn't just kissing her; he was asking questions she had no hope of answering; he was taking her places she had never been and had no intention of going.

But she was going there.

No. She was Jill Shaw, solidly grounded nursing director of Crocodile Creek hospital. She recalled it with a tiny gasp of shock. Her hands shoved between Charles's chest and her breasts and she pushed back.

He released her immediately, leaning back so he could see her in the moonlight. He looked as surprised as she did, she thought shakily. As out of his element. The great Charles Wetherby, shocked.

'I don't think…' She tried and then had to try again for her voice came out a squeak. 'I don't think this is a good idea.'

'Kissing?'

'Anything,' she managed. She was still squeaking. Oh, for heaven's sake… She was a mature woman. It had just been a kiss.

Yes, but what a kiss. If a kiss could wipe a woman's logic away as this one had… If a kiss could make her feel beautiful…

She wasn't beautiful. She had to get her bearings. She had to be sensible.

'We don't want anything to happen?' Charles queried, and she bit her lip.

'Certainly not.'

'Any particular reason?'

'We're too old.'

'Hey! Speak for yourself.'

'I didn't mean…' She swallowed. 'Charles, maybe I need to say… I just don't want…' Another swallow. Another attempt. 'I'm not going to be what you might call a jealous wife. I don't know what you do now…'

'For sex, you mean?' he asked, and affront had given way to bemusement.

'I don't need to know,' she said hurriedly. 'I mean… I don't even know…'

'If I can?' he said, still bemused. 'I can.' Damn him, he was enjoying her discomfiture.

'That's…that's good. I guess. So if you want to…'

'If I want to then you'll permit it? But not with you?'

'Just because you kissed me doesn't mean I'm expecting…'

'What if I want to?'

'You don't want to,' she said flatly. 'Or, at least, I don't. Look, it was a very romantic evening, for which I thank you. I love my ring.' She glanced down at it, a moonbeam caught it at just the right angle and she saw fire. 'I really love my ring. But what we're doing is practical.'

'You don't find me—'

'Don't ask,' she snapped. 'It's ludicrous.'

'Of course it's ludicrous,' he said, and the trace of laughter died from his voice as if it had never been.

What…? Oh, God. 'I didn't mean that,' she whispered, mortified.

'Of course you didn't.' He turned back to the wheel and flicked the engine into life. 'Don't worry. I won't touch you again. It's time we were home.'

'Charles…'

'It's OK,' he said wearily. 'As you say, we're too old. Let's go and pick up Lily and tell her she has two very respectable prospective parents.'

Jill shrank back into the passenger seat and felt about six inches tall. She'd never meant to infer she found Charles's disability offensive. Or even a bar to…well, to anything.

It was just that she didn't want anything. She didn't want contact at all.

She surely didn't want to risk those sensations coursing

through her that threatened to undermine the control she'd fought like a wildcat to regain after her marriage. She never wanted to be exposed again.

She should apologise to Charles. His face was set and grim, and she could lighten it. She could make him smile.

But…but…

Did she want him to smile? Not when they were alone, she thought frantically. Not when she was dressed like this, when she was wearing his ring. Not when his smile made her feel vulnerable and exposed and terrified.

No. Better to sit here, rigid, on the far side of the car, to school her expression into passive nothingness.

Like a cold fish.

She'd heard one of the younger nurses call her that once, and she'd thought, Good. That was how she wanted to be thought of. Emotional nothingness.

But she had a daughter. Or she'd have a daughter once this marriage took place. How could she be a cold fish with a daughter?

'Keeping ourselves only unto ourselves except for when we're with Lily,' Charles said.

'You understand,' she whispered, humbled.

'We're birds of a feather,' he said.

'Charles, I am sorry.'

'Don't be sorry,' he said. 'It was me who kissed you. I was overstepping the boundaries. It won't happen again.'

Lily was asleep when they arrived at Cal and Gina's. Cal heard the car and brought her out to them. She was slight for her age, a wiry, freckled imp with a tangle of brown-gold curls and a smattering of freckles, just like Jill's. She woke as Jill buckled her into her car seat but she made no demur. She was accustomed to this. Even when her parents had been alive, their love affair with rodeos meant she was very adaptable.

'Goodnight, sleepyhead,' Cal said, ruffling her tousled curls before he stepped back from the car. Then he smiled at Jill. He lifted her ring hand and whistled.

'Congratulations.' He hugged her and kissed her on the cheek. Jill found herself flushing.

'It's nothing.'

'It's fabulous,' he said. He looked into the car at Charles and grinned. 'Congratulations to you, too.'

'Thanks,' Charles said. 'But we're only doing it for Lily.'

'Right,' Cal said, sounding dubious. He looked back into the car at their sleepy little daughter. She was wearing her favourite pink pyjamas with blue moons and stars, her curls were tied up—or they had been tied up—with a huge, silver bow and there was a smudge of green paint on her nose.

'We did give her a bath,' he said ruefully. 'With CJ. And Gina did her hair.'

'I'll give her another one before she leaves tomorrow,' Jill said.

'You're not coming across to the island for the opening?'

'I'm in charge here.'

'Alistair can take over. You know he'd like—'

'I'm in charge here,' she said flatly.

'But you're telling Lily tonight, right?'

'Telling me what?' Lily asked sleepily.

'What we've been doing tonight,' Charles said bluntly from inside the car. 'Come on, Jill. I need to go back to the hospital before I go to bed. I have two patients I want to see tonight and there's packing to do afterwards. We need to move.'

So move they did. They took Lily home and tucked her in as they'd done a score of times before this night and Jill thought, Where do we start?

Lily started for them. She snuggled into her little bed, checked that her toys—two teddies, one giraffe, a bull like her favourite real bull, Oscar, one duck and a doll with no hair—

were all lined up in their appropriate places. Then she said, 'It's a really pretty ring. Did Charles give it to you?'

'Yes,' Jill said, and felt helpless.

'Why?'

'We've decided to get married,' Charles said. 'You know your uncle came today? He says he wants you to live with a real mother and father. For some reason your Uncle Tom thinks that we can only be a real mother and father if we're married. Jill and I want to look after you until you're old enough to take care of yourself. So we've decided to get married so your Uncle Tom will let us keep you.'

She regarded them both, her eyes wide and interested.

'So you'll look after me all the time?'

'Yes,' Jill said firmly. 'If it's OK with you we'll sign papers that say no one can take you away from us.' She took a deep breath. 'And, Lily…if you wanted to call us…well, maybe you wouldn't want to call us Mum and Dad. Your mum and dad were your special, real parents. But if you feel you'll like to maybe call us something like Mama and Papa…'

'Your names are Jill and Charles,' Lily said flatly.

'That's right,' Charles said, and he flicked a strand of Lily's hair back behind her ear. 'We're Jill and Charles, or whatever you want to call us. And you're Lily. But we're family from now on. Right?'

'OK,' Lily said obligingly, and hugged her teddies and closed her eyes. 'Goodnight.'

And that was that. A mammoth, life-changing decision converted to a few simple sentences. They returned to Jill's living room and Jill felt deflated.

The door from her living room led through to Charles's living room. This was what they did every night. They said goodnight to Lily. Charles wheeled through to his apartment. He closed the door behind him.

Contact over.

'You know, we could knock this whole wall out,' Charles said thoughtfully, and she stared at him.

'What?'

'This used to be an old homestead before the hospital was built. It was too big for me so I cut it into two apartments. But this room… It was the original sitting room. It had huge French windows looking over the cove. I had to sacrifice the windows to convert it into two rooms. We've knocked a door through. Why not go the whole hog, knock the entire wall down and put the windows back in? You know we almost always have the televisions on the same channel. Or we could have stereo televisions. Or,' he said, warming to his theme with typical male enthusiasm, 'one really big television.'

'I might have known,' she said tightly. 'Boys with technology. Is this the entire motivation behind the proposal?'

'Hey, you get an opal,' he said, aggrieved. 'I reckon I ought to get a big screen. How big do you think, if we make it one room?' He hesitated. 'A family room,' he said cautiously. 'Where we can be a family.'

'But I need my privacy.'

His smile died. 'I'm not talking combining bedrooms, Jill.'

'No,' she said, and faltered.

'So marriage doesn't mean watching telly together. It doesn't mean family?'

How to explain that that was dangerous in itself? Closeness? Familiarity? She didn't do it.

As it was, it sometimes felt too close. Lily popped back and forth between the apartments. She slept in her bedroom on Jill's side, but if Jill was caught up at the hospital Charles would check on her. Jill would occasionally get home and discover Charles on her side of the beige door.

It shouldn't matter. But she'd spent so long building her defences that to breach them now…

Kelvin was there. He was still in her head. A shadow, waiting to crash down on her. She should see a therapist, she thought dully, but then a therapist would tell her she was imagining her terror, and she knew she wasn't.

She was risking enough with this marriage. If she could just keep it…nothing, maybe the sky wouldn't fall on her head.

'OK, we won't knock down the wall,' Charles said wearily. 'We go on as before.'

'Maybe I could buy you a bigger television,' she said, striving for lightness.

'I guess I can make that decision on my own,' he said flatly. 'I need to get over to the hospital.' He hesitated. 'Jill, I'm intending to be on the island for two weeks. I've agreed to take Lily and she's looking forward to it. But Cal's right. You could come over. Come to the opening ceremony at least.'

The opening… Half the press in the country would be converging on the island. Photographers. Media. No and no and no.

'I said I'd take over here.'

'We can cover you. Hell, Jill, you can organise the roster for you to be gone. You've done half the planning for the new rehabilitation centre anyway. You've cut all the red tape. You've negotiated with the Health Commission. It's your baby.'

Should she explain it was because she was still afraid of Kelvin? After eight years? He'd say it was crazy.

It was crazy.

'It's your dream, Charles,' she said at last.

'We're allowed to share dreams,' he snapped, and she blinked at the anger in his voice.

'I… Yes,' she whispered. 'But there's no need for me to be there.'

'You can stay in the damned resort if you want,' he snapped. 'It's on the far side of the island from my bungalow.'

'That's dumb.'

'It is dumb, isn't it?' he said. 'But it's what you seem to want. Jill, I'm not going to pressure you, but if you act like I'm an ogre…'

'You kissed me.'

'So what?' he said explosively. 'You're an attractive woman, you've just agreed to marry me and I kissed you. Obviously it was a mistake. I've agreed it won't happen again. But Lily needs a mother and a father. As far as I can see it, that's not going to happen if we live on separate planets.'

'Charles—'

'Just work it out,' he said wearily. 'Figure out the rules and let me know what they are. Meanwhile I have patients to check. Go to bed. I'll see you in the morning before I leave.'

He spun his chair and pushed it through the dividing door, back into his side of the house.

He closed the door behind him.

CHAPTER FOUR

WHY had he kissed her? Had he learned nothing? Charles wheeled himself through the silent corridors of the hospital and decided he was worse than a fool.

This was an eminently sensible solution as to what to do for Lily. To stuff it with emotion…

It was just that she was so damned kissable.

See, that was the problem. He hesitated at the nurses' station. He needed to get the patient notes for old Joe Bloomfield. He lifted them from the rack but then sat with them on his knee and stared down unseeingly at the closely written information.

Jill was gorgeous.

Under that prickly exterior he'd always suspected there was a woman of passion. He knew her past had never left her. He knew she was fearful to the point of paranoia.

That she'd agreed to marry him was extraordinary. She'd let him put his ring on her finger and the pleasure in her lovely grey-blue eyes had made him forget momentarily that she had years and years of carefully built defences in place.

And then he'd kissed her and for a moment she'd responded. For a moment he'd felt the woman he'd suspected she could be. Warm, vibrant, passionate. A woman to cherish.

Only then…remembrance had flooded back and the shutters had slammed down. How the hell he'd thought he could get through her reserves… He was a paraplegic, for God's sake.

He swore. There was a rail running the length of the corridor, used so patients returning to mobility could practise their walking with something to grab. He spun his chair up to the rail, flipped up his footrests, grabbed the rail and hauled himself up.

He stood, gripping the rail fiercely with both hands. Slowly, his left hand gripping so hard his knuckles showed white, he released his right hand and turned slightly so he was facing forward. Hell, his legs were useless.

But not completely. He had some feeling. He had some strength. He pushed his right leg forward, steadied, and then brought the left one through. His toes didn't pull up on command so it was more of a shuffle. He could do this on the walking frame or on elbow crutches but to do it one-handed…

He was going to do it.

He took another step and then another. Beads of sweat were standing out on his forehead. Dammit, he'd get to the storeroom.

Another step. Another. Another.

He reached the boundary of the door where the rail gave out. He swung in and allowed himself the luxury of gripping the rail with both hands.

Applause came from behind him. He turned and Susie, the hospital physio, was watching him.

'If all my spinal patients had your determination I'd be out of a job,' she said cheerfully. 'How long have you been doing that?'

'Do you mind?'

'Sneaking up on you? Not at all.' She beamed. 'It's your specialty, I know, so it's nice to catch you out at your own game. Do you want your chair?'

He'd intended to walk back, but that would involve turning his left hip outward. His left hip wasn't as obliging as his right.

'Yes, please,' he said, and she pushed his chair forward. He sank into it with relief.

'You've already done an hour and a half in the gym today,' Susie said mildly. 'Plus swimming. You don't think maybe you're pushing it?'

'No.'

'And you're thinking of getting married.'

'I'd imagine they know it in London by now,' he said sourly.

She chuckled and leaned back against the rail. 'Charles, do you ever see a specialist any more?'

'No,' he said, revolted.

'You treat yourself, huh?'

'There's nothing they can do for me.'

'Hey, there's stuff I've done for you,' she retorted. 'Isn't there? Go on, admit it. Since you started working on the exercises I've recommended you're a lot more mobile.'

'Blowing your own trumpet…'

'If I don't, no one else will,' she retorted, still smiling. Then her smile faded. 'You damned near snapped my head off when I suggested it, but the exercises I've given you have worked. And you'll probably snap my head off now, too.'

'Then don't suggest anything.'

'Well, I won't,' she said. 'It wouldn't be appropriate. I'm your employee, I'm several years younger than you are, and I'm a single woman. But I am a trained physio. You know, if you're about to be married—'

'Susie!'

'There's things that can help,' she said, speaking fast and backing away. By the look on Charles's face she *needed* to back away. 'I know there are. Exercises that can make things much more fun for you and Jill.'

'It's a marriage of convenience.'

'I know that,' she said scornfully. 'The whole town knows you're doing it for Lily. But we also know that you guys are lovely people. A real live marriage would be fantastic for both of you and if it's for want of a few exercises…'

'You want to be turned off without a reference? Shipped

off to Weipa on the next plane out of here, with instructions to send you down the deepest mine? Susie, butt out.'

'I'm butting,' she said, but she grinned as she turned and headed back the way she'd come. 'I've said what I want to say. I know names and I can give you contact details. In fact, you might find them on your desk even without me asking. You employed an interfering, bossy physiotherapist who always wants the best for her patients. That's what you got, Dr Wetherby, so live with it. See you on the boat tomorrow.'

She headed out the nearest exit as a jar loaded with pencils came flying down the corridor after her.

Packing for Lily took ten minutes. Jill managed to stretch it out to half an hour.

Her brain was on empty. It was like she'd been shocked into a stupor. How many pairs of knickers? She stared into the depths of Lily's bureau and her brain didn't come up with an answer that made sense.

She'd agreed to marry Charles.

He'd kissed her.

Her fingers kept drifting up to her lips as if they were bruised. They weren't. It hadn't been a punishing kiss. It had been a kiss of exploration. A kiss of questions.

And she'd answered those questions. She thought back to the look on Charles's face as she'd said it was ludicrous.

Of course it's ludicrous.

He'd thought she'd been backing off from him because his legs didn't work properly. As if that could possibly make him less than sexy.

And that was the whole problem. If he wasn't so sexy maybe she could give a bit. She thought about Charles's suggestion that they knock the wall out between them. They could sit here like some aging Darby and Joan, watching their telly into their twilight years.

Now, there was a ludicrous suggestion. Charles with a

crocheted rug over his knees, twiddling with the remote control? No and no and no.

Charles.

She lifted her hand so she could see her ring. Its flames flickered in the light cast by Lily's bedside lamp, seemingly almost a living stone.

He'd known she didn't want a diamond. He'd given her this.

Involuntarily she raised the ring to her lips. To be given something so beautiful… It was as if she had worth.

She did have worth, she told herself harshly. For heaven's sake, of all the miserable, self-indulgent thoughts… She was really competent at her job. She ran the nursing administration with a skill she was proud of.

She'd make a good mother to Lily. She knew she would. She had to stop Kelvin's ugly taunts messing with the rest of her life.

She crossed to the bed, stooped and lifted a strand of dusty curls from across Lily's eyes. From across her daughter's eyes.

'You have us both,' she whispered to the sleeping child. 'It'll be good.'

It'd be better if she let Charles knock down a wall.

She couldn't. She just couldn't.

She went back to staring at the knickers drawer but nothing was happening. Finally she shrugged and went out to the phone.

Mrs Grubb answered on the first call.

'Dora, can you do your knitting in front of my telly instead of yours for an hour?' she asked. Dora Grubb was the hospital cook and babysitter to any child she could get her hands on. She had five grown sons, not one of them had produced a grandchild and she was suffering. She was also a lady who lived on snatches of sleep, regarding eight hours in one hit as a waste. For two medics with a little girl who needed company at a moment's notice, Dora was a blessing.

'Sure,' Dora said expansively. 'I'll be there in two minutes. I wanted to get this sleeve finished tonight. And this is special after all.' Jill could practically hear her beam. 'Grub's telling me you and the doc—'

'We're engaged,' Jill confirmed hastily. 'For Lily's sake.'

'But you and Doc already went out tonight, yes?'

'I… Yes.'

'I guess you want to take a walk in the moonlight or something,' she said, sounding hopeful.

'Something,' Jill said. 'It's a full moon. The road will be clear. I'm going to run to the bridge and back.'

'Run…tonight… Are you out of your mind?'

'If I don't run I will be out of my mind,' Jill said firmly, and she put the phone down on Dora's romantic imaginings and went to put her trainers on. Running was what she did when her brain was threatening to explode. It was threatening to explode now.

Hopefully Charles would come back while she was out. He'd look through and find Dora. That'd be the end of any romantic imaginings as far as tonight was concerned.

Hopefully he wouldn't look through again. And tomorrow he was going to the island. Without her.

Maybe her brain wouldn't explode just yet.

The boat was due to leave at eleven. Jill was on duty from seven. She was up at dawn, finishing Lily's packing. Lily woke just as she finished and she sat down on the bed and hugged her, keeping her voice low. Charles would be up already, doing his admin stuff in his living room next door. Or packing himself.

Their normal routine was that he worked here until it was time for Lily to go to school. This morning Lily wasn't going to school—she was heading to the island with Charles. Jill could stay here until she left—the hospital was quiet enough for her to take a few hours off—but she wanted to be out of here.

'I'll come and wave to you at the boat,' she said. 'You get up now and have breakfast with Charles.'

'I thought you said he was my daddy now.'

'OK,' she said, regrouping. 'You go in and have breakfast with Daddy.'

'I'll go in and have breakfast with Charles,' she said contrarily, and submitted to Jill kissing her goodbye.

OK. Work.

Maybe she should say good morning to Charles, too. She didn't usually. But…she was wearing a ring.

She stuck her head round the dividing door. As she'd thought, Charles was up and working already. He was sitting by the small window where he could get a glimpse of the sea. It really would be sensible to haul this whole wall out. If they did that…

She looked at him before he raised his head. He was intent on what he was doing, his intelligent face focused. He worked so hard for this place.

He should have his view if he wanted it.

But…

'I didn't think you'd be working this morning,' he growled, and she jumped a foot.

'Hell, Charles…'

'What?'

'You scared me.'

'It's my principal skill,' he said, and smiled at her, but his smile didn't reach his eyes. 'You're not walking us down to the boat?'

'I thought I'd go through the checklist with Gina one more time,' she said. They had some really sick kids going to Wallaby Island this time. Usually they selected their kids with care so there would only be one or two high-risk participants, but the newly vamped kids' camp was set up with a state-of-the-art medical facility. The influx of doctors into the region over the last few years meant they could rotate enough doctors out of Crocodile Creek here to have a skilled team on the island at all times.

They had three precarious asthmatics going this time, a

couple of kids with advanced cancer, two brittle diabetics…
Each kid had to be given a good time, not cosseted but allowed
to enjoy the tropical experience to the full. But they also had
to be covered every medical eventuality.

Jill and Charles had gone over the equipment lists so many
times they must have covered all bases.

'It'll be fine,' Charles growled. 'You know that.'

'I just want to check.'

'You mean you're feeling weird being here. With me.'

'You kissed me,' she said, not accusing. Just a statement
of fact.

'I did, didn't I?' he said, and this time the smile did reach
his eyes. 'And very nice it was, too. OK, go check your drugs.
But be down at the chapel at nine-thirty.'

'The chapel?' she said, startled.

'I should have asked you that, too,' he said, but he didn't
sound apologetic. 'You were out running when I came back
last night and I had to get this set up. We need to be married
in a month. That means we have to give four weeks' legal
notice. The only person around here I know who does marriages is the local vicar. If we want a civil ceremony we need
to go to Cairns and we can't get to Cairns today to sign our
statements of intent.'

'You've found this out…when?'

'By talking to Bill McKenzie this morning,' he said. 'As it
happens, Hannah Blake died in the night. I went over to say
goodbye and Bill was already there.'

He would be, Jill thought. Bill McKenzie was Crocodile
Creek's only clergyman. Little and round and overwhelmingly
kind, pushing seventy, he beamed at the world over his too-
thick glasses. He welcomed all comers, regardless of relig-
ious affiliation, and if there'd been a death and a need Bill
would have sensed it before being asked.

'He said to come over before the boat leaves and he'll get
it sorted.'

'Bill's going to marry us?' she said cautiously.

'He'll do the paperwork. If you won't want a church wedding we can take our paperwork down to Cairns.' He hesitated. 'I don't mind. But then…' He smiled again. 'It's my first wedding. I wouldn't mind doing it here. Maybe I should even wear white.'

'Where I should wear purple as a tainted woman.'

'That's a bit melodramatic,' he said. 'But if you want purple…'

'Charles…'

'Whatever you want, Jill,' he said, becoming serious. 'But we do need to get these legalities sorted.'

They did. Fine. But…signing this morning…

'You can always pull out later,' Charles said. 'You're not marrying this morning. You're simply signing a document of intent. And I swear I won't sue if you don't go through with it.'

'Your white bridegroom gear might be really expensive,' she said, struggling for lightness. 'I hear veils for men cost a fortune.'

'You reckon I should hold in reserve my right to sue?'

'Let's both hold it in reserve,' she said. 'Meanwhile, I'm heading over to check medical lists.'

A document of intent. That was all it was, Charles thought. But sitting in the vestry of Crocodile Creek's little chapel, waiting for Jill, he suddenly felt as nervous as a bridegroom on his wedding day.

What if she pulled out?

She had every right to pull out. And why should he mind?

Because of Lily.

This was more than Lily.

He felt his fingers dig involuntarily into his palms. He wanted this.

Damn, his palms were sweating.

'She'll come,' Bill said, smiling sympathetically at him. 'This is Jill we're talking about.'

'She's terrified of marriage.'

'She is,' the elderly priest agreed. 'She's been on the outside looking in for a good while now. But, then, so have you.' He smiled. 'And here she is. Running. She's always running, your bride. Maybe the pair of you will slow down a bit now.'

'I hardly run,' Charles said, but the priest simply smiled again and crossed to open the door for Jill.

She was wearing her work gear. Plain black trousers and a sleeveless white shirt. Plain black sandals. She'd tugged her hair back, as she always did, into a tight bunch at the back.

But she was beautiful, Charles thought. She was mature and assured and lovely.

Sure, she'd had it tough. She had life lines round her eyes. She was smiling, grasping Bill's hand, warm and friendly. Charles had seen her with patients in distress. Sure, she was matter-of-fact and practical, but patients responded to her. What you saw was what you got. A woman of integrity and courage and...

Beauty.

She deserved someone better than him.

She glanced across at him and her smile died. They stared at each other for a long moment while Bill looked on with bemusement.

In the end it was Bill who broke the silence.

'Well, my children,' he said gently, 'they tell me there's a boat about to leave. And they also tell me you want to get married.'

In the end it was relatively painless. Forms, forms and more forms. Legal stuff.

The emotional stuff could be put aside.

'You know, at this stage I normally give my couples a spiel about what marriage is all about,' Bill said as he collected the forms together.

'We know it,' Jill said.

'Do you?' Bill asked.

'As much as we need,' Jill said grimly. 'It's a marriage of convenience.'

'Is it a marriage before God?' Bill asked. 'You know, if you're intending to dissolve the marriage the moment Lily's of age then I can't marry you. Yes, I'll send the forms in and I'll organise for you to have a civil ceremony elsewhere. But if you're to have me marry you, then you're marrying for ever.'

'I…' Jill faltered and looked at Charles.

'I'd like to be married by Bill,' Charles said, and he met her confused gaze steadily. 'And I've no intention of marrying anyone else. As far as I'm concerned, it's for ever.'

'You won't want me hanging round you for ever.'

'I'm pretty used to you now,' Charles said softly. 'I'd miss you singing in the shower every morning.'

'I don't…' She paused. Oh, wait. Maybe she did.

'It's great,' Charles said, and he smiled.

She wished he wouldn't. He took her breath away. That she was agreeing to marry a man who smiled at her like that…

'Is it for ever, Jill?' Bill was asking gently, and she gave herself a mental shake. So what if it wasn't? She'd made these vows before. Sure, she'd had her father standing behind her with a metaphorical shotgun, but she'd made the vows and she'd broken them. What was different now?

Was she going into this intending to divorce?

Not yet.

'There's no one else I want to marry,' Jill said, almost in a whisper, and Bill looked at her sharply.

'Things change. People change. If you meet the man of your dreams…'

'I don't have dreams,' she said flatly.

'Neither do I,' Charles said dryly. 'So there you have it, Bill. Two pragmatic people without dreams, marrying to keep Lily safe. It seems we're both happy to have it in church—if you'll have us.'

'So you'll be promising to love, honour and obey?'

'Honour,' they said in unison, and Bill grinned.

'Well.' He considered them both, with affection and years of wisdom. 'I guess there's worse start-off points than that. You'll need to work out your own vows.'

'Can we do that?' Jill said cautiously.

'Sure,' he said, ready to be expansive. 'The way I'm looking at this—love comes in all shapes and sizes. I'm thinking love might be edging into the equation here, like it or not.'

'Not,' Jill snapped.

'We'll see,' Bill said, still smiling. 'Now, let's get these forms signed so you can catch the boat. Jill, I gather you're not going across to the island?'

'I need to work here.'

'You're promising to be a family,' he said, sounding disapproving for the first time.

'After the wedding.'

'So be it.' He sighed, and then smiled again. 'Lots of marriages have started with less and gone a lot further. Let's get you started and see where you end up.'

CHAPTER FIVE

MAYBE she should have gone. Jill stood on the jetty and she could still feel the warmth of Lily's small hand in hers. She could still see Charles's smile. If he hadn't been on elbow crutches as he boarded the boat he might have even kissed her goodbye, she thought, but she'd been able to back away.

She wanted no more kissing.

'You take care of yourself,' he'd said as he'd left her. 'You're my affianced wife. You're not to work too hard, you're to delegate anything you don't want to do, and if I come back and find you're tired I'll sack the entire Croc Creek medical team.'

He'd said it loud enough for everyone on the jetty to hear. There'd been grins and laughter from everyone and Jill's colour was still fading. For Charles to make such a public statement of affection...

It warmed her inside, but it also made her feel disoriented. People were watching her as if she was different. She wasn't different.

She couldn't be different.

'You take care of yourself—and of Lily,' she'd managed, and Charles had smiled at her with a tenderness that had been a caress all on its own.

And then they'd gone.

She watched them until they'd rounded the headland out of the cove. Two distant figures in the stern of the boat.

Charles seated, Lily standing beside him. They waved to her just before they disappeared from view.

Her husband and her daughter.

She let the words seep into her head, waiting for the familiar sense of panic to reassert itself. Strangely, it didn't.

It was because they weren't here, she thought. They were away for maybe two weeks.

She should join them.

That did make her panic. Marriage…families…were all very well in the abstract. But reality…

Charles was so different to Kelvin.

That made her flinch. The thought of Kelvin.

Where was he? If he knew what she was doing now, what she intended…

Kelvin was no more to her now than a distant nightmare, she told herself. A bad dream. He was so far out of her world that he should no longer exist.

But he'd always said…

No. She didn't have to listen to the echoes of her past. This was the future.

A future she was scared to embrace.

There was a roar of an engine behind her. A motorbike came down the jetty's service road, leaning over so far Jill flinched again. Georgie. The town's obstetrician. Biker extraordinaire.

'Have I missed them?' she yelled, dumping her bike and striding along the jetty to meet Jill. 'Damn. I wanted to say goodbye but the Langley's baby wouldn't co-operate. Charles must be feeling so proud.'

'He is,' Jill said.

'And not just because of the island,' Georgie said, and grinned and tucked her arm into that of her friend's. 'Another wedding! Hooray.'

'Yeah.'

'Hey, you don't sound like a blushing bride.'

'I'm a bit old to be blushing,' Jill said bluntly, and Georgie hesitated. Like Jill, Georgie had had it tough in her early years. Now blessedly in love with her ultra-conservative Alistair, the look she gave Jill said she understood a bit of what she was going through.

'Charles is a lovely man,' she said gently.

'He wouldn't thank you for saying it.'

'Yeah, he likes us to think he's omnipotent and crabby,' Georgie agreed, and chuckled. 'But you know he's a pussy cat.'

'Right,' Jill said faintly.

'You *do* want a pussy cat?' Georgie said cautiously. 'Women like us…it's so easy to think we can never be happy unless we're with someone who knocks us round.'

'I don't—'

'No, but my Alistair's a case in point,' Georgie said, pushing on. 'If he hadn't turned into hero material the day of the cyclone, I might never have seen what he was.'

'I don't need Charles to be macho.' Jill sniffed. 'I mean… maybe he already is.'

Georgie paused. She released her friend, turned and faced her square on.

'Hey! You think he's a hunk?' she said on a note of discovery. 'Don't you?'

'I… Of course. I mean, don't we all?'

'Maybe not in the way I'm seeing in your eyes,' she said thoughtfully. 'Wow.'

'I don't want to think of him like that.'

'Why?'

'It scares me to death,' Jill said flatly. 'As if I can ever get away from my past.'

'You're still frightened of your ex?'

'He always said…' She shook her head. 'No. It's crazy. After so many years…'

'Follow your instincts,' Georgie said urgently. 'Talk to someone if you're frightened. Talk to the police.'

'There's no need.' She shook herself. 'No. This is stupid.

No policeman would ever agree I have reason to be afraid. It's paranoia and it's dumb. I'm a really practical person and we're going into this marriage for purely practical reasons. Stop distracting me. I need to get on.'

'Fine,' Georgie said, and linked arms again. 'Let's get on. But this is very exciting. Something tells me Sister Jill Shaw's armour plating might not be as impermeable as once supposed. And now he's left. Absence makes the heart grow fonder, they say.' And then as Jill shoved her friend sideways on the jetty, pushing her inexorably towards the water, she broke free, laughing.

'Enough. There's crocodiles in this creek and I have babies to deliver. And you have a wedding to arrange. Can I be bridesmaid?'

'No.'

'I'll ask Charles,' Georgie said, refusing to be squashed. 'This is a wedding, after all. You guys need to get a consensus. I think I want to wear red.'

Wallaby Island was fantastic.

The work that had gone into this place since the cyclone was truly astounding. Charles had been back on the mainland for the last two weeks. He'd hoped the final stages could be done without him.

They had.

The contractors had done him proud, as had his medical staff. Beth, his newly employed doctor in charge, showed him through the facilities as soon as he arrived. Charles was mostly silent as he wheeled his way through the ten-bed hospital, the individual bunkhouses, the family units, bungalows with every facility for looking after an ill child.

Everything was ready. His team was in place, even down to the wildlife guides and recreational officers who had been recruited specifically to give ill children a wonderful time. They all had first-aid qualifications and they'd spent the last few weeks increasing that training. If a child started feeling wheezy on a nocturnal wildlife hunt, it would never go unnoticed with these leaders.

'It's fabulous,' he told Beth.

'It is, isn't it?' she said. Then, as a crazy, woolly mutt of a dog came bounding out from the bushland behind them, she chuckled. 'And here's Garf, to greet you.'

'Garf,' Lily yelled, delighted. Garf was the camp dog, a great golden labradoodle with a grin the size of a house. He'd been purchased because of his friendly nature and his hypoallegenic fur. He went happily from kid to kid, seeming almost to sense which kids needed him.

But Lily loved him best of all. Maybe they could get Lily her own dog, Charles thought as he watched Lily hug and Garf lick. If the wall came out…

Dumb thought.

'I need to be getting back,' Beth said, glancing at her watch. 'One of the rangers rang in to say he's coming down with flu. I agreed to meet him at three.'

'Can I help?'

'No,' she said, and smiled. 'The one thing I don't need at the moment is medical help. Every medic who's ever worked at Croc Creek seems to have taken the grand opening as an excuse to visit. There's a huge medical conference over at the eco-resort as well, and they're all aching to check out the new facilities. I have doctors coming out of my ears. If I'm not careful I'll find myself sacked because I'm redundant. I'm only going back now to assert my rights to treat the odd patient myself.'

So he wasn't needed.

He was needed. It was just…his role here was administrative. That was what he did.

But he watched Beth until she disappeared from view and thought that's where he wanted to be. In the middle of the action.

'When are the kids coming?' Lily asked, and he forced his attention back to his daughter.

'Tomorrow.'

'That's good 'cos I need someone to play with.'

Ditto, he thought, and then gave himself a metaphorical sideswipe to the head. One kiss and he'd been thrown right out of kilter.

Jill wasn't coming over.

He had a ceremony to organise.

He might resent his administrative role, but it produced results. As soon as the kids arrived—disabled and chronically ill kids from all over Australia—his team swung into action like a well-oiled machine, a machine with heart. The island came alive with the sound of kids having fun.

For the privileged few staying at the five-star eco-resort at the far end of the island, this must seem a normal camp for normal kids. It was only when you got closer and saw the prostheses, the wheelchairs, the oxygen cylinders, you might suspect things were not quite right.

This was the culmination of Charles's dream. It should feel fantastic. It did feel fantastic, Charles thought as the camp settled into its intended rhythm. So why did it feel empty?

Lily had been on Wallaby Island a dozen times already. She blended in with the camp kids like she belonged. Too easily, Charles thought as the days wore on. She should have roots.

She should have Jill.

Hell, Jill should be here.

On the third night the camp recreational officers set up a campfire and barbecue on the beach. It sometimes seemed more trouble than it was worth, getting onto the sand—dry sand was incredibly difficult to negotiate, even on elbow crutches—but there was no way he'd stay isolated while the rest of the camp had fun. Besides, it was something of a tradition and several of his staff had come over to attend from the mainland.

Jill was the isolated one, he thought as he watched the kids toast more marshmallows than they could possibly eat. Claire

Harvey was eating her third. That mightn't seem a great deal, but nine-year-old Claire had become anorexic after the death of her mother. By the look on her father's face, the third marshmallow was a very big deal indeed.

They were getting through to Claire. Could he get through to Jill?

He was seated a way back from the fire—far enough to make a phone call without being disturbed. On impulse he made the call. Jill answered on the third ring.

'Charles.' Her voice lifted in apprehension. 'Is something wrong?'

'What should be wrong?' he asked. Normally when he phoned she slipped straight into business mode. Why the change?

The kiss?

'I… Sorry,' she said, sounding flustered, and he knew that indeed it was the kiss. 'What can I do for you?'

'We're missing you,' he said. 'Lily and me.'

There was a sharp intake of breath. Whatever she'd expected, it hadn't been that.

'Don't,' she said sharply.

'Don't miss you?'

'Say things you don't mean. Lily doesn't miss anyone.'

He winced. Maybe it was the truth, though. Lily was having fun down by the shallows, romping with Garf, surrounded by kids and carers. But as he watched…

'I think she does need us, Jill,' he said softly. 'I think she surrounds herself with people and activity as a form of defence. Like you surround yourself with work.'

'I'm not marrying a psychologist,' she snapped, and he chuckled.

'I wouldn't be a very good one. Jill, come over.'

'I… I can't.'

'You can,' he said inexorably. 'I'm your boss. I know every detail of every staff roster and I say you can.'

'I don't want to.'

'Now, that's a different matter,' he said gravely. 'Do you want to tell me why not?'

There was a drawn-out silence. He let it lie. In the course of years of being medical director he'd learned the importance of not rushing to fill the silence. And Jill, of all people, mustn't be pushed.

'Charles, I need a bit of time to get my head around what's happened,' she confessed at last. 'When Wendy suggested this…'

'I believe it was me who suggested marriage.' That seemed suddenly important. He wanted no marriage at the instigation of a social worker.

'Well, it seemed a good idea. It seemed logical.'

'It is logical,' he agreed. 'I do think we needed to make a decision. We've kept everything in limbo for too long, and that's not good for anyone, let alone a child.'

'You know I agree,' she said, sounding suddenly desperate. 'And it still does seem logical. But then…the ring…and you kissed me…and then you suggested we knock down the wall…'

'We can take the ring back,' he said gravely. 'We can keep the wall. There's not a lot we can do about the kiss.'

'I'm being dumb,' she said miserably.

'Jill, I'm not coercing you into this against your will.'

'Of course you're not,' she said hotly. 'You're a good man.'

He didn't feel like a good man. He felt like throwing the damned phone into the sea.

Hell, what was happening here? Talk of a wedding and suddenly he was seen as noble.

What was he doing, marrying like this? He didn't want to. When the hell had what he wanted ever come into it?

'Charles, I need to go,' Jill said, sounding distracted. 'Jack Blake's come in bleeding all over my nice clean tiles. I need to find someone to put a couple of stitches in.'

'Do you want to end this?' he asked. He knew Jack. Jack

required stitches approximately once a month. He really did have to learn how to whittle something other than his fingers.

Jack's stitches could wait for a bit. This was important.

'N-no.'

'You're still wearing the ring?'

'Yes.' Her voice firmed. 'It really is beautiful. Thank you, Charles.'

'I don't want your gratitude,' he said savagely. 'I need your commitment. Think about it and let me know.'

He left Jill to Jack's stitches, and he was left to his thoughts. They weren't great. All around him were kids and parents and carers. They were having a good time or giving a good time. They had roles here.

He hated the reality that he couldn't join in. He had the reputation for being aloof, and of knowing things almost before they happened. That wasn't hard. He was always on the fringes, looking on. He could see tension between people. He could see people simply living.

He let his mind drift back to when he'd been a young man, to when he'd still had legs that had held him up. He'd always been in the thick of things. He'd loved life. Hell, he still did. That was part of the reason he'd worked so hard to build this place. To show kids with disabilities that they could join in.

A great example he was being, he thought morosely, giving himself a mental shake and looking around for Lily. It was time they headed back to the cabin.

She wasn't with the other kids, playing down by the water's edge.

Great. Here he was, being a parent, caught up with introspection and not watching his daughter.

He grabbed his elbow crutches and pushed himself to his feet so he could see further. She was nowhere in sight.

'Luke,' he called to the closest doctor he knew. 'Where's Lily? She was here just a minute ago. Dammit, I hate it when she runs off in the dark.' She did it too often, he thought. She'd be with the other kids and then simply disappear. Like she didn't need people.

But she hadn't gone far. Luke walked into the shadows, calling, and she re-emerged almost at once. She came toward him, carrying something with care.

She seldom went far, Charles thought. It was simply that she was independent. Too independent, he thought grimly. Maybe that went for the three of them. Jill and Lily and…and maybe him, too. Could three isolated units become a family?

'I need to show Charles,' she was telling Luke. 'He'll help.'

'I don't think…' Luke said doubtfully, but she shrugged him off and came running over the sand toward him. He sank back into his chair and turned his attention to what she was carrying.

A dead bird.

'Look. It's sick.'

'It's dead,' he told her.

'Can you make it alive?'

'Lily, no.' It lay limp in her hands. When he put a tentative hand on the bird's soft neck he felt the last faint traces of warmth. 'It's still warm. That means it's only just died, but it is dead. Put it down on the sand, Lily.'

'But can't you make it come back alive?'

'Lily, I'm a people doctor, not a bird doctor, and anyway it's dead. I can't bring it back.'

'But I saw it move.'

'You probably did,' he agreed. 'It must have been its last flutter. It hasn't been dead for long. But it is dead now, I promise, and there's nothing we can do. Luke?' Again he had to turn to his fellow doctor, and again he didn't like it.

'Bury it?' Luke suggested. 'I think we'd better. We don't want the kids playing round with it.'

It was a wedgetailed shearwater. Charles lifted it from Lily's hands and gave it to Luke with a feeling of regret. The shearwaters were beautiful birds, migrating all the way from Siberia during the Australian winter and coming back every year to breed on the island. He handed it over to Luke with a feeling of vague disquiet.

'Go and wash your hands in the sea,' he told Lily, 'and then we'll do them properly with soap when we get back to the cabin.'

It was time to go. He and Lily had this down to a fine art. He got back on his elbow crutches. Lily turned his wheelchair back to front and towed it across the sand to firmer ground. He followed as fast as he could, but Lily was patient. She didn't mind waiting.

Strangely he didn't mind Lily helping him. A six-year-old…his daughter.

She was subdued, and she stayed subdued when they reached their cabin. Still uneasy about the bird, he insisted she have a bath. She allowed him to tuck her into bed but she was obviously still concerned about her bird.

'Why couldn't you make it alive again?' she asked. 'You're a doctor.'

'There are some things doctors can't make better.'

'Like your legs?'

'That's right.'

She thought about it. 'So when you and Jill get sick and die…I'll have to live with someone else?'

That was one to give him pause.

'Lily, you were very, very unlucky that your mum and dad were killed.' He didn't know where to go with this. He wanted, desperately, for Jill to be there. 'I think you can be pretty sure we'll be around until you're grown up.'

She wasn't convinced. 'Can I live with Gina and Cal if you die?'

Maybe now wasn't the time for probabilities. 'We won't die.'

'You're in a wheelchair. You're already sick.'

'I've explained that to you. I even showed you the model of the spine I have in my office. I have a small damaged part of my spine that controls my legs. The rest of me's fine.'

'Yes, but you'll get worse,' she said, definite. 'I think Gina and Cal will look after me.'

'Gina and Cal would look after you if we did die,' he said, stumped for anything else to say. 'Anyone in Croc Creek would. But they won't need to.'

She wasn't hearing reassurance. She was focused on security. 'They're all my friends,' she said doubtfully. 'But Uncle Tom didn't want me. Maybe they won't want me either.'

'Jill and I want you. We love you, Lily.'

'Yes,' she whispered, as if it made no difference at all. 'I'm going to sleep now.'

She wiggled over in bed and turned her face to the wall. He had been dismissed.

He went and sat on the veranda and stared out to sea. He hadn't got that right.

What were he and Jill doing? he thought bleakly. How could they make a family from three such troubled pasts?

Jill rang just before midnight. He was still sitting on the veranda. Filling time. If Lily wasn't there, he'd be at the hospital, getting things done. It drove him nuts to be still.

If Jill were there, he could be gone.

'Don't tell me,' she said as he answered his phone on the first ring. 'You're sitting on the veranda, bored out of your brain, I knew it. I thought I'd check but I knew it.'

'I'm about to go to bed.' But he was absurdly—disproportionately—pleased she'd rung before he had.

'You live on four hours' sleep a night and now you're stuck caring for Lily. You'll be going stir crazy.'

'I'm fine,' he said. No one else gave him a hard time like Jill did. No one knew him as Jill did.

'A bit of enforced idleness will do you good,' she said. 'You've been pushing yourself.'

'Is that another reason for you not coming over?'

'I don't need another reason. I'm busy.'

'You're still on duty?'

'I told you—yes.'

'And no one else can work instead. Jill, I need you here.'

There was a moment's silence. 'Why?' she said at last.

'Hell, Jill, we're getting married.'

'That's no reason for you to need me. What else has happened?'

'Lily found a dead bird.'

She didn't respond. She was like him, he thought ruefully. He'd learned not to fill silences—to wait for others to jump in. Jill was turning his trick neatly on him.

'It led to a discussion of who'll look after her when we die,' he explained at last, giving in to the inevitable. 'She's pretty sure we'll end up dying. Tomorrow, if not sooner.'

'Do you think that's why she's so eager to be friends with everyone?'

'I don't know.' He raked his hair with his fingers, exasperated. 'I'm in uncharted territory here, Jill.'

'Which is why you want me to come over?'

'Yes,' he admitted bluntly.

'And to get you off the veranda and back into the hospital.'

Was he so transparent?

'I'm taking thinking time,' she said into the silence.

'You feel you've been rushed?'

'Maybe.'

Anger washed across him like a vicious slap. Anger and frustration. 'Look, if you really don't want this then put the blasted ring in the rubbish and get on with your life,' he snapped, and this time the silence was loaded.

'Charles, can you please try and understand?'

'I'm trying. But I'm being played the villain here. Coercing you into marriage against your will. Adopting Lily when I've already got one foot—or one wheel—in the grave.'

'Are you sure that's what she thinks?'

'I don't know what she thinks. I don't know what you think.'

'I'll try and come over for the opening.'

'That's big of you.'

'It is,' she said abruptly. She paused, obviously fighting for control. 'Look, I know, I'm being unfair, but there's baggage I need to sort out. I hoped you'd be understanding.'

'I'm trying,' he snapped back. He took a deep breath. 'I'm sorry. I know you do have issues but I have the odd one or two myself. This seemed pretty clear cut when we first discussed it. If it's not then we need to pull back. Lily's been messed around enough. Neither of us want pressure, but both of us want what's best for Lily. Maybe…' He hesitated.

'Maybe what?'

'Maybe given both our backgrounds we're not what Lily needs. Maybe we should face it.' He stared out to sea and what he was saying seemed to be forced out of him, a leaden fog of reality. 'Maybe Lily needs parents who know what loving's all about. Maybe she needs parents who can reach her.'

'You're saying it's unfair of us to adopt her?'

'I don't know,' he said heavily. 'It seems, however, that we both have time to think about it.'

He clicked his phone closed.

'Thinking sucks,' he added to the silence. 'Who wants to think?'

But in the end the thinking stopped. In the end, Jill came. Not because Charles wanted her to, but because Lily was ill.

The Friday before the opening Lily woke up lethargic and not wanting breakfast. Actually, Lily seldom wanted breakfast but that was because she was aching to get outside and see what the day had to offer.

On Friday morning she fiddled with her cornflakes, wandered over to the settee and curled up, uninterested in anything.

Alarmed, Charles checked her out. She seemed OK. Maybe she was coming down with a cold.

She stayed listless. He spent most of the day with her,

aching to be at the hospital, aching to be working instead of reading Lily stories or simply watching her watch television.

'You can go and look after the sick kids,' she said mid-afternoon, and he thought he'd been summarily dismissed.

'I like being here.'

'No, you don't,' she said wisely. 'You keep looking out the window.'

'But it's my job,' he said. 'To stay here and look after you. That's what dads do.'

'You're not my dad.'

'I'd like to be.'

'Mmm,' she said, noncommittal. She watched a bit more television, then drifted off to sleep.

Charles called in one of the hike leaders to sit with her while she slept. There was a mass of stuff happening down at the hospital in preparation for tomorrow's opening. He should have been down there all day.

What sort of medical director was he?

A medical director with a kid of his own.

There was a drama with a teenager with a split chin. He reacted with gratitude—any medical need helped keep him from thinking about the personal issues battering him from all angles. Sadly—or fortunately, depending on whose angle you looked at it from—the parents refused to allow him to take care of it. They were hyper-caring parents, they wanted a plastic surgeon on the job, and amazingly there was a plastic surgeon available among the parents and dignitaries.

When Charles returned to the cottage Lily was awake.

She was feverish and beginning to be obviously unwell.

It wasn't just a cold.

He examined her with care. She was running a temperature of thirty-nine, she had swollen lymph nodes, she was dry and fretful.

She curled into herself as she always did when she was hurt. She wanted no comfort.

'Lily, you need to drink,' he told her, but she'd have none of it. Neither would she tolerate him giving her a sponge bath.

'I think you should get someone to fly Jill over here.'

Beth, the permanent doctor in charge of the Wallaby Island clinic, had come across to check on Lily when Charles had been caught up in the chin drama. As Lily whimpered into her pillow, a picture of abject misery, Beth placed her hand on the little girl's forehead and frowned across at Charles, sending him a silent message of concern. 'You'll be OK, sweetheart,' she said. 'It'll be just a nasty virus that's made you feel bad. But what if we ask Jill to come?'

'Jill won't come when Charles is here,' Lily whispered.

Was the conflict between them so obvious? Or... Charles thought back to the months Lily had been living with them. This was the pattern, he thought. One of them did the caring while the other worked.

Other families spent their spare time together, he thought with a flash of useless insight. Not them.

'The boat won't get over here until late tomorrow,' he told Beth, feeling useless.

She fixed him with a look. Hell, what was it with the women here? The minute he'd put the ring on Jill's finger he'd lost his authority.

'You know, you *are* the medical director and founder of this entire set-up,' she said now. 'You call the shots. There's a helicopter parked here right now. Mike Poulos is here for the opening and he's more than ready to fly back to Croc Creek. The only reason the chopper's here is that Mike's using this as a base for his runs because he wants to attend the opening. You know that. Jill could be here in little more than an hour.'

'It's just a virus.'

'You're her dad, Charles,' Beth said gently. 'You're the only dad she's got. What do they say about doctors' kids getting worse treatment than any other segment of the population? Do you think Lily might feel better if Jill was here?'

Maybe not, Charles thought. He could set up a drip if needed. He could do anything Lily required.

But…

But he'd feel better if Jill was there. He'd feel better if they made the attempt to make this family unit work. Even if Lily didn't need it.

Maybe she did need it, though, he thought, watching Lily as Beth smoothed a curl back behind her ear. She reacted to everyone but clung to no one. Maybe it was time to teach her to cling.

Maybe that clinging had to start now.

'OK, we need Jill,' he said in a tone that startled both Beth and Lily. He knew it and he grimaced. It was his medical director tone—the voice he used when he wanted things done. But now the decision had been made, he needed to get on with it. 'Lily, possum, drink your lemonade while I phone your… While I phone Jill.'

'You called me possum,' Lily said, puzzled.

'Do you mind?'

'You always call me Lily.'

'I guess. Sorry.'

'I like Possum,' she said, and then she sighed. 'My neck hurts.'

Her neck. He gave Beth a startled glance and wheeled across to the bed. 'Is it stiff?' he asked. He ran his fingers gently down the sides of her neck and watched as she winced. But surely it wasn't the stiffness that might be a sign of meningitis. Surely it was only her glands, swollen even more than when he'd last felt them.

'We'll give you some medicine to make it stop hurting,' he told her. 'And then you can go to sleep. If we're lucky, by the time you wake up Jill will be here.'

'Where will she sleep?' Lily asked, but Beth was lifting her so she could drink her lemonade. Lily spilt a little and it distracted her enough for Charles not to have to answer the question.

But it was a good question, he thought as Beth bade them goodnight and headed back to the hospital. The island accommodation was booked to capacity.

This was a one-bedroom cabin. Lily was sleeping on the settee in the living room. The settee was tiny. There was a bedroom at the clinic used by visiting specialists. Charles usually used that when Jill came across, or when their cabin was needed, but it was being used tonight by visiting dignitaries.

Maybe he shouldn't ask her to come.

But he was asking her. If they were to be a family…family started now.

He tucked the sheet around Lily, frowning as he felt the heat of her skin. She was only in her knickers and he'd covered her in a sheet and nothing else, but still she was hot.

He wanted Jill.

CHAPTER SIX

SHE arrived three hours later. He heard the chopper come into land. Not wanting to leave Lily, he simply wheeled out to the veranda to wait.

Ten minutes later she came hurrying up the bushland path, carrying her overnight bag. A tiny wallaby grazing in front of the cabin stopped its feeding and moved a generous two feet to the left to let her pass. Wallaby Island was aptly named. The wallabies thought they had right of way.

But Jill wasn't focused on wallabies. She climbed the steps two at a time, her face tight with anxiety.

'How is she?'

'We're looking at a cold,' he said, frowning. He hadn't meant to scare her. He thought he'd outlined exactly what was wrong.

'No,' she said tightly, reaching the top step and looking down at him. 'You said it was just a cold, but you wanted me to come.'

'Lily wanted you to come,' he said, and then could have bitten his tongue as he heard the echoes of his words and saw them resonate. Jill's face tightened. 'I didn't mean that,' he said swiftly. 'It was just… Yeah, she's ill and miserable. She's running a fever, her glands are swollen. She's a sick little girl. But she's still drinking and the blood test Beth ran shows her electrolytes are fine.'

'So why—?'

'I asked her if she wanted you. She said you wouldn't be

here if I was here,' he told her. 'I thought…' He paused, unsure where to go from here. But suddenly, dammit, he was going on. 'We need to be a family, Jill,' he said gently. 'I know you're unsure but that decision has to be made and I guess I'm asking you to make it now. Though maybe you have already made it. When I phoned and said Lily was ill, you weren't asking how ill, you were already thinking about how to get here. You're her mother in every way but legally.'

'I am,' she said uncertainly. She flipped her hair back behind her ears in a gesture he recognised as pure nerves. 'I need… I need to see her.'

'Of course you do,' he said, and smiled, trying to lighten things. He wheeled across to the screen door and hauled it open. 'She's asleep but I think we should wake her. Families start now.'

'Let's not make this heavy,' Jill retorted.

'Let's not.'

Lily woke when Jill touched her. That in itself was unusual. Lily usually slept the sleep of the angels. She had two gears, Charles thought, full throttle or at a dead stop, but now she was in between, exhausted enough to sleep but too feverish to sleep deeply. She opened her eyes as Jill stroked her hair, and her eyes widened with astonishment.

'Jill.'

'Hi, sweetheart,' Jill said softly. 'I'm sorry you're feeling bad.'

'You came.'

'I came. I hated thinking you were sick without me.'

'Charles said I have a virus. He said I have to keep drinking lemonade.' Her voice was a thready whisper, and Jill lifted her wrist and held it.

She glanced across at Charles and Charles wondered if she was getting worse.

'Lemonade's good,' Jill said.

'Mrs Grubb made it.'

'It's lucky the Grubbs are here,' Jill said, stroking her hair.

'Everyone's here for the opening,' Lily whispered. 'Do you think it was the bird that made me sick?'

'I don't think so,' Jill said, startled.

'Charles said I had to wash my hands 'cos we didn't know why the bird died. But it did die.' Her eyes widened again, flaring in panic. 'I might die.'

'Well, you won't,' Jill said solidly. 'The sad thing for the bird was that it didn't have a bird doctor to care for it. You have a people doctor right here—you know Charles is a lovely doctor and he makes people better all the time.'

'And you're the boss nurse,' Lily said, her panic fading.

'I am,' Jill said. 'And what I say is what happens. So I'm saying I need to give you a sponge bath. We'll see if we can stop you shivering. And then we'll give you some more medicine and you can go to sleep while we wait for you to get better.'

'You'll both look after me?'

'Yes.'

'You'll both stay here?'

The implications hit her. Charles saw the moment Jill realised what had been gnawing at him since he'd decided to ask her to come. She glanced through to the bedroom. Charles's gear was on the left-hand side of the big bed. There was nothing on the right.

'We're both staying here,' Charles said strongly, before she could answer. Dammit, he'd sleep in his wheelchair on the veranda if he had to. But they were both here for Lily and nowhere else.

Lily submitted to Jill's sponge bath. She even seemed to enjoy it. The paracetamol took hold and before Jill had finished her eyes were drooping closed.

Charles had been sitting in the background, watching. As Lily slept he wheeled across to the kitchenette, made a couple of mugs of tea and carried them out to the veranda.

Jill settled Lily to her satisfaction and came out to join him. There were two cane chairs out on the veranda, one at each end. Charles had pushed his wheelchair to rest by one, the mugs of tea on the table in front of him. Jill cast a fleeting glance at the other chair and Charles thought if she had a choice, that's where she'd sit.

She was like a frightened kid.

'I'm not going to jump you, Jill,' he said softly, and she flushed and came and sat in the chair beside him.

'I know. I'm being dumb. I'm sorry.'

She was still wearing the ring. That was a good sign. A very good sign.

'It…it seems more than a cold,' she ventured.

'I know. I'm starting to worry.'

'You don't think we should put her in hospital tonight?'

'She's still drinking. As long as we keep her cool and hydrated, there's not a lot of point.'

'You're sure it's viral?'

'There's nothing to explain a bacterial infection. I've given her a thorough check.'

'It's come on fast.' She hesitated. 'You're sure it couldn't be connected with the dead bird?'

'I doubt it,' Charles said, thinking it through as he spoke. In truth he was starting to get edgy. Lily had brought one dead bird to camp. So far today Charles had seen more than a dozen dead birds on the beach and a couple on the paths leading up to the bungalows.

It'd simply be nature taking its course, he told himself. The shearwaters' normal migration patterns might have been interrupted by something similar to the cyclone. Their nesting burrows might have been destroyed, and for ill and struggling birds, coming back to a burrow that had to be rebuilt might well mean physical exertion they were simply not capable of.

'You're worried about the bird,' Jill said.

'I'm worried about Lily.'

'No one else is ill?'

'We've got a couple of kids down with colds. And one of the rangers.'

'Just colds?'

'It was just a dead bird, Jill.'

'Yes, but this isn't just a cold.'

'Let's see how she is in the morning,' he said uneasily. 'If she's still unwell, I'll run some more blood tests.'

'You have the opening tomorrow night.'

'Yes.' He grimaced. It promised to be a glittering black-tie occasion at the resort hotel. It wasn't something he'd planned but there were so many firms eager to be corporate sponsors for such a worthy cause that it had been impossible to keep this low key.

'So did you bring your tux?' she said, teasing.

'My dinner suit,' he growled. 'Bloody thing.'

'You look great in it.'

'Right,' he said dryly. 'Seeing the only time I'm in it is for weddings… You want me to wear a dinner suit to ours?'

'No!'

'That's unequivocal.'

'It is,' she said, biting her lip.

'So what do you want me to wear?'

'Charles…'

'You want to call the whole thing off?'

'I… No.'

'What do you want to do?'

'Just leave everything as it is.'

'It's not going to happen, Jill. We'll lose Lily.'

'Maybe Tom will change his mind.'

'Will you go down to Brisbane to ask him?'

'He won't change his mind,' she said miserably.

'I guess he won't.' He hesitated. 'So what are you afraid of?'

'I'm not afraid.'

'Is my paraplegia a plus or a minus?' he asked bluntly.

'What do you mean?'

'Are you not wanting to marry me because I'm in a wheelchair? Or is the fact that I'm in a wheelchair making it seem safe for you to marry me?'

'I guess…mostly the second,' she whispered.

'That's honest at least.'

'I know you well enough now to figure I need to be honest.'

'You also know me well enough now to cut it out with the whispering,' he retorted. 'The Jill Shaw I asked to marry me is a feisty, strong-minded woman who doesn't suffer fools gladly, who doesn't put up with rubbish and who knows what she wants in life. She'll be a great mother for my daughter. The Jill who's emerged since I put a ring on her finger, though, is a pale imitation of that. For heaven's sake Jill, you're almost a trembling virgin.'

'I can hardly be that,' she said, startled.

'It's what you sound like.'

'I didn't mean—'

'Then cut it out,' he snapped. He set down his mug with a decisive thump. 'I'm going to bed. This is the time you start whimpering with fear and insisting I sleep on the veranda or decide to sleep in an armchair by Lily's bed. But there's a perfectly comfortable bed which is big enough for both of us. Whimpering aside. You want to share a bed with me?'

'I…'

'No whimpering.'

'I wouldn't whimper.' And indeed the whimper had faded. She sounded affronted.

'Good. You want me to sleep on the veranda?'

'Where?'

'In my chair,' he said. 'It's not the first time I've done it.'

'Of course I don't. But I should…'

'You can if you want,' he said cordially. 'Stretched between two cane chairs. You'll be as uncomfortable as hell, and I'll think you're even more wimpish. But go ahead.'

'Charles—'

'And, no, I'm making no more promises about not jumping you,' he said. 'No more reassurances. You either trust me or you don't.'

He left her. He wheeled inside. She heard him in the bathroom, brushing his teeth. Ordinary. Mundane.

The problem was, though, she thought fearfully, that Charles was none of those things. From the time she'd first met him she'd been mesmerised by the power of his personality. And by his physical power, too, she thought. The sheer strength of the man... She watched him day after day as he hauled himself out of his chair and forced his body through the exercise routine he imposed on himself. A lesser man than Charles would have given in to his disability. Not Charles.

He wasn't the giving-in type.

He was waiting for her in the bedroom.

If she had been in her twenties again... If she had been young and gorgeous...

Maybe she'd jump him, she thought ruefully. Maybe she could show him just what a fantastic marriage they could have.

But she was just Jill. The practical one. Nurse administrator, oldest nurse in the hospital, plain and even a bit saggy next to the gorgeous young medics Charles worked with every day.

He was stuck with her because he wanted Lily. So to be afraid of him...

It wasn't that she was afraid of him, she thought. But she was afraid of showing him just how attracted she was to him. Dammit, she didn't want him feeling even more sorry for her.

He'd finished in the bathroom.

They were getting married. There was one bedroom. One bed.

What were her fears? That Kelvin would find them? That somehow by loving she put Lily and Charles at risk?

That she wasn't good enough for them?

'Ugly cow.' She heard Kelvin's taunt echoing over and over.

Well, she thought, maybe she was and maybe she wasn't. But the lights could always go off. Charles didn't have to look at her. If she could give him pleasure…

Maybe…just maybe…

Come on, you ugly cow, don't be a wimp, she told herself. Just for tonight…just for Charles, try and be beautiful.

As if.

But it was a thought and it wasn't a bad thought. In fact, it wasn't bad at all.

A wallaby was watching her from below the veranda.

'Can I do it?' she asked him.

He didn't say no. That was enough.

'I'll do it if he wants,' she told the wallaby. 'I can't say fairer than that.'

She took a deep breath and headed inside.

He was already in bed. Or on the bed. He was wearing plain, blue pyjama pants and nothing else.

The man was in his mid-forties. He should be showing signs of wear and tear by now. A trace of flab.

There wasn't the slightest sign of flab about him. He looked… What did the younger nurses call it…ripped? Buffed, in the old parlance.

Sexy in anyone's vernacular.

How did they describe it in the penny dreadfuls? In walked Doctor Sex-On-Legs. Nurse Ditzy took one look at the hunk in the white coat, her knees turned to jelly, her heart pounded wildly and she had to lean against the wall to stop herself from swooning.

She grinned.

'So what's funny?'

'The changing face of medicine,' she said obliquely. 'You don't wear a pyjama top?

'I'm wearing pyjama bottoms in deference to you. I'm hoping you have a flannel nightgown to match.'

'T-shirt and knickers,' she said. 'I travel light. Close your eyes, roll over and face the wall, and I'll put them on.' She hesitated. 'No. I'll put them on in the bathroom. But face the wall anyway.'

'On account of T-shirt and knickers would inflame my senses.'

'There'll be no inflaming of senses in my bedroom,' she said primly.

'I seem to recall it's my bedroom.'

'What's yours is mine. It's in the wedding vows. Face the wall.'

'Yes, ma'am.'

It was all very well facing the wall. It was another thing entirely going to sleep.

Charles wasn't a great sleeper at the best of times. If Jill hadn't been there he'd probably still be out on the veranda, catching up on clinical journals, or over at the hospital, making himself useful. Or, hell, even reading a decent whodunit.

Instead of which he was facing the wall while his intended bride lay three feet away.

As far to the other side of the bed as she could get.

Was she asleep?

He lay and listened to her breathing. Strong and even, strong and even…

Nah. She was as wide awake as he was.

'Should we tell each other bedtime stories?' he asked, and she gasped.

'I…'

'I knew you weren't asleep,' he said in satisfaction. 'No one breathes as regularly as that unless they're really concentrating.'

'It's my way of going to sleep,' she said with dignity. 'I feel my breath.'

'You feel your breath?'

'You know Gabby? She teaches relaxation classes to our expectant mums. Our insurance doesn't cover her unless there's a trained health professional in attendance so I've sat in a few times. She teaches the mums to focus on each breath. In. Out. If I can't feel my breath above my lip I'm doing it wrong.'

Charles breathed in and out a few times. Harder.

'Nope,' he said. 'It's not doing it for me.'

'So how do you go to sleep?' She sighed. 'No, you don't have to tell me. You don't. You disappear about bedtime and then appear again and scare the living daylights out of unsuspecting night staff.'

'If they work in my hospital they pretty soon aren't unsuspecting,' he said in satisfaction, and she relaxed enough to chuckle.

'No. Your reputation is truly fearsome.'

'Is that why you're scared of me?'

'I'm not scared of you.'

'See, that's what I don't understand.' Despite her previous orders he rolled over in bed so he could see her in the moonlight. 'I would have said you were the only member of my staff who's never been in awe of me. No matter how grouchy I get.'

'Which is pretty grouchy.'

'See what I mean? You give cheek.'

'I can't help myself.'

'So where's the cheek disappeared to?' he asked gently. 'Why have you turned into a trembling kid?'

'Hey!'

'A trembling kid,' he said firmly, 'who looks as if she'll flinch if I raise my hand, rather than raise her hand right back.'

'If I thought you'd ever hit anyone, I'd never come near you.'

'You do believe that?'

'I…I guess I do. Did I tell you that you were allowed to turn over?'

'I decided I was allowed to turn over all by myself,' he said proudly. 'I'm a big kid.'

'You're no kid,' she whispered into the dark.

He didn't know what to say to that.

A trembling kid…

Did he really think that of her? She needed to get a grip, she thought. Here she was, lying in bed with the man of her dreams…

Hey, she was! The thought was suddenly mind-blowing in its intensity. It was like she'd been creeping round the edges, not seeing, and suddenly the sky had opened, revealing all. Or, more like, slapping her over the face like a wet fish.

Wow, she thought suddenly. And then, more awesomely, Wow!

She was in bed with Charles.

She should go back to concentrating on breathing techniques.

But why?

A tiny little voice had started shouting from inside her head when she'd been out on the veranda. Her inner voice was getting louder by the second.

You're in bed with Charles, the voice was saying. Just shut up with your dithering, you idiot, and do what you really, really want.

Was there a reason why not?

Probably there were lots of reasons. Millions of reasons. Control, for one thing, but then again, maybe that was fear as well. More of the trembling-kid thing.

He wouldn't cross her boundaries. She knew that. And she also knew that she'd implied those boundaries were there because he had a damaged spine.

Which was dumb. But if he thought it…hell, she hated that he could think it.

So what to do about it?

She knew what she could do about it. But…

But don't think about it, she decided, squashing her dumb scruples way back into the furthest recesses of her brain. Thinking turned her into a bag of nerves.

Just do it.

What was happening? He was lying staring into the dark, tense as hell, trying to figure where to take it and how, and—

'How long since you've had sex?' Jill suddenly asked into the stillness.

The stillness suddenly got…well, suddenly a lot more still.

'Did you ask what I just thought you asked?' he managed.

'Yep.'

The rising moon was sending soft light washing across the bed. Jill was staring up at the ceiling, her face almost expressionless. But not quite. There was a tiny upward quirk of her lips, as though she knew the shock her words would cause. It was almost a look of…mischief?

Jill?

'I can't see that it's your business,' he started, and there it was again, that definite quirk. Like she'd decided, Dammit, she'd crossed some line and she wasn't going back.

'We're getting married, aren't we?' she said. 'So maybe it is my business.'

'But you said…'

'That we had to keep our distance. I did think that. Maybe the sensible part of me still does. But there's a tiny, nonsensible part of me that's saying if we're going to cross boundaries anyway… If you're going to knock out that wall…'

'I said we didn't have to.'

'So you did,' she said cordially. 'And then you invited me into bed with you.'

'Because we had no choice.'

'So you don't want to make love with me?'

'I didn't say that,' he managed. Just.

'You inferred it.'

Silence fell again. Charles stared across at her, baffled. Surely she didn't mean…

'I can, you know,' he said, as if goaded, and she nodded.

'You said you could. Your injury's below L2. What sort of sensation do you have?'

'Most.' He hesitated. 'Or I assume most. I forget…'

'What it was like to be nineteen and blind with lust?' she queried, as if this was a totally normal conversation, as if she was speaking to a teenage patient about his physical difficulties. 'I'd imagine back then you weren't thinking, Oh, I must remember how it feels when someone's finger runs the full length—'

'Jill!'

'Hey, I'm just talking,' she said, and rolled over and propped herself up on her elbows so she could look down at him in the moonlight. The mischief was there in full now. Her eyes were alight with laughter.

He couldn't believe what he was hearing. Jill. Prim, proper, self-contained Jill, who kept herself to herself.

'It is a blur,' he admitted. 'Not a bad blur…'

'See, the problem for me is that it is a bad blur,' she confessed. 'I haven't made love to anyone but Kelvin in my life. How appalling is that for an admission? He owned me body and soul. I was so much younger than him—the first few times I was desperate to please him, and after that I was simply trapped and he used me as he willed. But there were bits…' She paused, almost as if she couldn't believe she was about to say. 'There were bits I think could have been better. Things I wouldn't mind just trying…'

'But your boundaries…' To say he was hornswoggled was an understatement.

'I learned a long time ago that sex isn't a total loss of emotional control,' she said.

'You kept yourself apart in marriage?'

'Of course I did.'

'So you're saying we could…'

'Only if you want.'

'I guess I do want,' he said cautiously. Hell, of course he wanted. She was propped up on her elbows, smiling at him. Her beautiful curls were cascading softly around her shoulders. Her lovely grey-blue eyes were twinkling down at him, the laughter lines at the edges creasing, deepening the sense of surety, maturity.

Maturity? He wasn't feeling mature right now. He was feeling like a kid who'd been offered the moon.

'I'm not sure…'

'If you remember how? I'm not sure if I remember either. But if you want, we could give it a really good shot.'

'I want,' he said, suddenly definite, and she chuckled. It was a sound he'd very seldom heard. Sister Jill Shaw laughing. Sister Jill Shaw leaning forward to kiss him lightly on the lips.

Her curls fell onto his chest. They barely touched, a light feather brush. It was the most erotic feeling he'd ever known.

She let her head fall to rest on his chest. Her hands moved.

His whole world seemed to still.

'You're a very sexy man, Charles Weatherby.'

Yeah, right. But this wasn't the time to argue. 'You're pretty damned sexy yourself,' he managed—but only just. For lightly, so lightly that at first he thought surely he must be dreaming, her fingers were drifting down, along his chest, lower, across the flatness of his stomach. Lower still. To touch…

His whole body shuddered in response and there it was again, that lovely, throaty chuckle.

'You are interested, then.'

'Are you kidding?' he breathed, and suddenly it wasn't Jill who was calling the shots. He had her in his arms, lifting her high so he could see her, all of her in the moonlight, then tugging her down against him. His body felt alive, strong, young. And so did she. She felt amazing. The loveliest thing… His hands slipped under her T-shirt. She was wearing no bra.

Her skin was silky smooth, so smooth that to touch her sent erotic shivers shooting through his body, and it was as if he was being jolted awake after years of sleeping. His hands cupped her breasts, marvelling at the perfection of her. She was lying on his chest. He rolled and she rolled with him so they were side by side. Her breasts moulded softly under his hands. Her nipples were proudly upright, making their own statement.

She was as aroused as he was.

She'd instigated this. She wanted it.

She was in his arms, a warm, vibrant woman. Jill. He'd suspected there was this under her controlled, almost fearful exterior, and he'd been right.

'You're beautiful,' he whispered into her hair. 'Jill, you're magnificent.'

'There's no need to get carried away,' she said, sounding embarrassed. And then… 'Mind, you're not bad yourself.'

'You've seen worse things come out of cheese?' he teased, and she chuckled again and looped her hands around his neck and tugged his face toward her.

'There's not a lot of things come out of cheese I'd kiss like I'm intending to kiss you,' she whispered. 'Or the next bit either, come to think about it. Charles, I'm fed up with this talking bit. Do you want to take me?'

'More than anything in the world,' he murmured and she smiled in the moonlight, a tiny cat-got-the-cream smile that did things to his body he hadn't known his body was capable of. The way he was feeling… It was like life was opening before him. Gates that had been slammed shut years ago were opening in the face of this woman's smile.

'I want you so badly I'm on fire,' she whispered, and that was enough. He found her mouth. He took her body tight against him and swung her over him. She lay atop him, her T-shirt soft against his skin.

She was struggling to get her hands free and he knew what

she wanted. He seized both sides of her T-shirt and it disappeared somewhere onto the floor.

She still had knickers on but she was attending to that herself. Dammit, if his legs worked properly he could kick off his pyjama pants.

He needn't have worried. Her knickers came off in one swift kick and then her fingers tugged his pants clear.

'Years and years of dressing patients,' she said smugly. 'I knew it'd come in handy one day.'

'You're playing nurse?'

'And you're playing doctor. Examining my breasts for lumps?'

'There seem to be two,' he said. 'Two magnificent…lumps. They need close examination.' He rolled sideways to flick on the bedside lamp but she was before him, pushing the lamp out of reach.

'No!'

'You don't want…'

'I do want. But dim is better.'

He frowned but she was having none of it.

'There's a lot here that needs close examination, and I can perform whatever examination I need to in the dark,' she whispered, her fingers closing in against his groin, making him groan in pleasure. 'As dedicated health professionals I suggest we get on with it. Right, Doctor?'

'Anything you say, Nurse,' he whispered, and chuckled and held her tight, glorying in the warmth of her, the smell of her, the taste…

Jill. This woman had promised to be his wife.

'I think I'm falling in love with my fiancée,' he murmured into her hair, and she chuckled and wriggled so her hair was brushing against his chest, over and over, in a motion that was unbelievably erotic.

'It's a pretty nice ring,' she whispered. 'It deserves a little love in the equation.'

'Are you saying—?'

'I'm not saying anything,' she said serenely, and her fingers moved again, searching, finding, sending sensations through his body that rendered him incapable of anything but the most primal needs. This woman in his arms, right now… This woman giving herself in a way he'd never dreamed she would. 'And why the hell are you?' she murmured. 'Talk, talk, talk. Charles, I don't want talking. I don't want thinking. I just want…you.'

CHAPTER SEVEN

JILL woke just before dawn. For a moment she struggled to remember where she was. All she knew was that she was enveloped in a cocoon of such intense pleasure that it was almost an out-of-body experience.

She'd made love to Charles.

She'd wanted to make love to Charles for years. She acknowledged it to herself now as she lay half-asleep, not wanting to open her eyes, not wanting this sensation to end. From the first time she'd seen him, when he'd interviewed her for the job, she'd thought simply that he was the sexiest man she'd ever met.

For those years she'd watched as medics—young men and women from around the world—lived and worked at Crocodile Creek. As romances happened around him. She'd watched Charles hold himself in rigid containment. She'd seen him at weddings, his eyes still. Perfectly disciplined.

He didn't want. He didn't allow himself to want.

As she had. But last night she'd relaxed the rules. Last night...

It had been so good. More than good. There wasn't a word for how he'd made her feel.

She'd read abut orgasms, but in truth she'd always believed they were something the popular press made up. A myth, promulgated by generations of women to please their men. *Yes, of course I came, dear, just like you.*

But it was no myth. Her lips curved into a smile of delicious remembrance. It was reality. Her reality.

She wiggled deliciously, loving the feel of the sheets against her bare skin. Hugely daring, she edged backward, thinking she'd curve against his body.

He wasn't there.

Her eyes flew open. She wiggled around, and Charles's side of the bed was empty.

The disappointment was almost overwhelming. For an appalling moment she thought, Had it all been a dream? But the indentation of his head was in his pillow. She touched the place where he'd been sleeping and it was still warm.

Maybe that's what had woken her. Charles getting up.

At least he hadn't seen her naked, she thought, but then… that was only a part of it.

His wheelchair was gone. She glanced round to the door. They'd left it open during the night so they could hear if Lily stirred. It was now shut.

She relaxed, just a little. She was familiar enough with Charles's routine to know he'd never sleep as long as she did. He'd have risen but he'd have wanted to leave her sleeping.

Self-consciously she tugged on her T-shirt and knickers and crossed to the door to see what was happening.

Charles was dressed. He was in his chair, seated by Lily's bed. Watching her sleep. He hadn't heard the door open. He was simply watching Lily.

His face said it all, she thought. No wonder he'd asked her to marry him. This was the child he'd never thought to have.

He wanted Lily as much as she did.

It should make her feel good. Strangely it didn't.

Last night…last night had been pure fun. Fun was something she had never had. The idea of loving as fun was novel and exciting. But it had been more than fun. Last night she'd given a part of her she'd never thought to give.

But Charles didn't really want to marry her. Oh, he'd enjoyed last night. She could keep giving him that, she thought. She could even take enjoyment herself. But she must never lose sight of the fact that he was marrying her for Lily's sake.

'How is she?' she whispered as he turned, his face snapping into a frown.

'I wanted you to sleep for longer.'

'I slept for longer than you.'

'About two minutes.' He smiled at her, and his smile raked her from the top of her head to the tips of her toes. 'I believe we were both very tired.'

'We worked very hard yesterday,' she said primly, and then gave in and smiled back. Wham. To allow herself to smile as she wanted to smile... She could see that she'd even surprised Charles. Well, she'd surprised him the night before. Why not keep on surprising them both?

'Lily's not great,' Charles was saying, dragging his eyes from hers with obvious difficulty. 'She's still running a fever.'

'You think we should wake her and get her to drink?'

'Let's leave her to have her sleep out,' Charles said. He ran his finger over the back of Lily's palm, pushing forward and watching the skin fall back into place immediately. It was a simple test but effective. If dehydration was a problem the wrinkles in the skin took a while to resettle.

There was a light knock on the door. Jill looked ruefully down at her bare legs, shrugged and went across to answer it. She'd be less respectable in a bikini, she thought, and anyone knocking at this hour had to be a friend.

It was. Beth was on the other side of the door, smiling a greeting.

'Hi,' she said. 'I was worried about waking you, but I was sure Charles would be awake.'

Only just, Jill felt like retorting, but she didn't. The whole hospital staff knew Charles survived on four or less hours of sleep a night. Last night he'd had, what, seven? In between interruptions. It was a piece of information she couldn't give Beth, but she did feel a trifle smug.

'I popped by to see how Lily was,' Beth said.

'No better,' Charles said, wheeling over to the door so he could be included in the conversation without risking waking Lily.

'We've got a couple more kids showing similar symptoms,' Beth said, looking worried. 'Fever, swollen glands, lethargy.'

'Our kids?' That was a worry. Normal kids like Lily could shake off a virus but the camp kids had other, deeper health problems. For Lily a virus was a hiccup. For kids with cancer or severe asthma, a virus could be a death sentence.

'All ours,' Beth confirmed. 'Their camp leaders rang me during the night on the report-any-symptom rule. I checked them out and ordered them to have a quiet day.' She hesitated, glancing over at Lily. 'Lily's the sickest.'

'She got sick first,' Charles retorted. 'Hell.'

'Look, let's not worry about it now.' Again Beth glanced from Charles to Jill. Noting Jill's bare legs. Noting the open bedroom door. Noting whatever else she fancied.

Jill's face was turning pink. She knew it was, but there wasn't a thing she could do about it.

'Would you guys like to go for a swim?' Beth asked, deliberately looking away from the bedroom door and making her voice bright and a bit too impersonal. So impersonal Jill knew she'd added up the evidence and was reaching her verdict.

'I might,' Charles growled, and Jill knew he was thinking exactly what she was thinking. That rumours were about to fly around the entire island.

'The day's going to be frantic,' Beth said. 'We've got the opening tonight. You'll be over run with every sponsor who's donated so much as an inch of newspaper space. You have a sick little girl and we have a couple of other sickies who may or may not prove to be worries. I'm coming off duty now. I need to eat breakfast and wind down before I go to bed. Your refrigerator is stocked with exactly the same ingredients as mine. I can eat breakfast here, listen to the dawn chorus from your veranda and keep an ear on Lily while you guys go swim off your energy.'

'I could go for a run,' Jill said, dubious.

'Or you could both go for a swim,' Beth said strongly. 'You know I'm the doctor in charge of this island. You also know the danger of swimming alone. I know, Charles, that you break the rules all the time, but I'm not aiding and abetting you. My offer is for you, Charles, to go for a swim while you, Jill, do what you want as long as it's within rescue distance of Charles.'

'I won't need rescuing,' Charles said, annoyed.

'Everyone needs rescuing some time or other,' Beth said enigmatically. 'I reckon you two are doing a pretty good job already. So my offer's on the table. Take it or leave it.'

Of course they took it.

Hard physical exercise was the best mental curative in the world, Jill thought as they made their way to the cove. On the flat paths around the camp Charles's wheelchair could go faster than she could walk. He'd slowed down. She wanted to run. He could keep up, she knew.

But running... She might not stop, she thought.

But the decision she'd made last night had been that she'd try to make this a marriage. That meant that somehow she had to leave the loner Jill behind. It meant she had to stop running.

Just a bit. Just when Charles was by her side.

'You don't want to go swimming,' he growled, and she jumped. The man was omnipotent. It was going to be unnerving spending a lifetime with a man who could read her mind.

'I don't mind swimming.'

'Run if you want.'

'I'm happy to swim with you.'

'I don't want you to be good to me,' he said grumpily, and

pushed his chair faster, forcing her to either break into a run or let him go.

She let him go. This was uncharted territory. She didn't have a clue how to react.

She walked on slowly, feeling foolish. When she emerged from the bushland to the little cove, Charles was already out of his chair, making his way to the water.

His chair wouldn't work on the soft sand. He was forced to use elbow crutches to get himself to the water.

He'd been incredibly lucky, she thought, to have been left with enough power in his legs to give him this much mobility.

She thought of last night and, despite her confusion, she felt herself smile. In that department he'd also been incredibly lucky. Or she'd been incredibly lucky. She was marrying him.

Last night could be the first night of many, and the thought was enough to take her breath away.

She felt herself blush. It was weird. She was out of her depth, losing control, but she wasn't panicking. In a sense it was like she was on the outside, looking in. Wondering what this strange, new Jill-person would do next.

She needed to swim. With Charles.

She hadn't seen him swim before. She knew that he did, but she also knew that he was a man who valued his privacy. She wasn't sure that he wanted her there now, watching him.

She should join him, but instead she tugged her T-shirt off, leaving only her bikini, then stood, feeling exposed and self-conscious. But distracted by Charles.

He used his elbow crutches until the waves were almost to his knees. The crutches were sinking into the soft sand but they were enough to give him the support he needed.

As the water reached knee depth he let himself drop into the shallow-breaking waves, then simply hurled the crutches up onto the beach. Then he sank full length into the sea and used his arms to pull himself out to deep water.

He was like a seal. He took less than a minute to reach the buoys marking the boundaries of the netted cove, slicing through the small, incoming waves with the ease born of long practice.

The power of the man took her breath away.

She hesitated, feeling unsure. This was so much his private territory. But he was beyond the breakers now, floating, looking back to the beach to see what she would do.

What did he think she'd do? Retreat?

What had he said? *I don't want you to be good to me.*

Sympathy was so far from what she was feeling that she almost laughed. Almost.

Her fiancé was waiting in deep water.

She was getting into some pretty deep water herself, she thought. But the time for retreating was past.

What the heck. Charles was waiting.

She tossed her T-shirt onto the sand and ran into the water.

In the water he was alive. He was free.

Every morning back at Crocodile Creek, Charles swam. There were so many small bays around Crocodile Creek that he could always find a private place to swim. Crocodiles usually only went to sea to transfer from one inlet to another, so as long as he stayed away from the mouth of the creek he was safe.

For the rest of the day his chair chafed him. He should be used to the restrictions by now, and mostly he was, but there were still many times when standing would be easier, walking would be faster, running would be fantastic.

But in the water his legs didn't hold him back at all. He had enough strength in them so they didn't drag, and the extra strength in his arms more than compensated.

Jill was watching him.

He wasn't sure what had happened with her last night, he thought as he swam. He'd accepted it with joy, but he wasn't sure that it was anything that could last.

He'd had so many people be good to him. Especially women. Men were gruff and taciturn and often embarrassed, but there'd been more than one woman in the past who'd approached him thinking…

Well, enough. He could feel sorry enough for himself without some damned do-gooder aiding and abetting the sympathy vote.

Had Jill made love to him out of sympathy?

He wasn't sure, he thought, not yet, but if she had then she'd done a good job of disguising it. Her turnaround had been astonishing. Magnificent.

Jill was magnificent.

He watched her run into the water. Her body was as taut and lithe as a teenager's. Years of running had toned her so there wasn't an inch of spare flesh on her.

What the hell was she doing, refusing to let him see her naked? But maybe…maybe it was because she didn't want to see him. Making love in the dark was possible.

No matter. He'd take Jill any way she offered herself.

She dived into the first small wave, and emerged spluttering. She didn't swim as often as he did. The waves here were tiny, the island sheltered from the bigger surf by miles of coral reef. But even this small wave was enough to make her splutter.

He smiled and stroked forward to meet her, sliding his body into a wave and riding it forward. He surfaced right by her legs and she was still wiping the water from her eyes.

He gripped her leg and she yelped.

'I'm not a shark,' he said, rolling over lazily and smiling up at her.

'You look like one to me,' she retorted, and then as the pressure on her leg grew greater she toppled forward into the shallows. 'Oi. Unhand me, sir.'

'Why would I?' he asked, teasing, and tugged her leg harder so she slid forward into his arms. Another wave broke over them. He lifted her high so she was clear of the water, and then brought her down again to kiss her.

'Charles…' she said, breathless.

'Yes?' He kissed her again, on the mouth, deeply, then sliding her upward so he could kiss the swell of her breasts.

'This is scaring me,' she managed.

'You don't seem scared.'

'No, but…'

'But what?'

'I didn't think… You must know I never intended last night to happen.'

'And I never allowed myself to hope it could happen,' he told her gravely, then had to lift her again to allow another wave to roll past. 'You know, if we're to make love here, we need to head further into the shallows. Or find ourselves snorkels.'

'We can't make love here,' she said, shocked.

'I guess it is more public than my little cove back at Croc Creek,' he said. 'How soon do you think we can go home?'

'You think…you really think we might…?'

'Why not?' he said, and tugged her down and kissed her again.

If she'd died and gone to heaven she couldn't feel any better than she did right now, she thought. He was kissing her, lifting her, kissing her again, laughing up at her, holding her in his arms so strongly she felt loved, protected, cherished. It was a surge of emotion so strong she could hardly take it in.

Another wave caught them, bigger than the rest. Charles's lifting techniques failed. He'd been holding his breath as the waves had passed but this one was too deep.

It submerged her. He let her fall. She fell into his arms, and they both emerged with noses and eyes full of water.

'Hey, you're no lifesaver,' she managed as she choked and choked again.

'Beth said you had to save me.'

'I can't save you if you try and drown me.' She chuckled and then looked at him through a mist of water and thought it was too much. She didn't deserve this. Even if he was doing it for Lily… To have this much happiness…

He was doing it for Lily. He had to be. But for now…

'Race you out to the buoy,' he said, and she stared at him in bemusement.

'Excuse me? You swim every morning. You'd beat me hands down.'

'Then give me a handicap.'

'One hand,' she said, and it was the right thing to say. People had been nice to him about his disability for so long that to insist on rules like this…

'Hey, I have no kicking power.'

'You have so,' she said serenely.

'I'd have to swim sidestroke.'

'Yep.'

'You'd have two good legs and two arms.'

'To your one arm. That might make us almost equal. Are you going to race or are you planning on thinking up more excuses?'

He stared at her. She stared back, challenging.

'Right,' he said. 'Ready, set, go.'

She beat him, but only just.

That required a re-race.

She beat him again, so she was handicapped. No kicking. That meant her two arms against his one.

He beat her for the next three races.

'OK, running tomorrow,' she gasped as they did the last of best out of five. 'Me against your wheelchair.'

'I'd beat you in a minute.'

'In a minute on sealed tracks, sure,' she said. 'I want all round the island on the unsealed tracks.'

'Hey! What about obstacles?'

'What's a few obstacles to you?' she teased, and watched with delight as his eyes lit up with laughter. She could make this serious man smile. She'd never tried. No one had. Everyone had always been in awe of him.

It was a shock. He didn't quite know how to take it. She wasn't sure if he'd keep on enjoying it, but it was working now and she intended to give it her very best shot. She'd keep on trying.

But he was glancing at his wristwatch, grimacing.

'We'd best get back,' he said regretfully. 'Lily…'

Of course. Lily. She'd almost forgotten.

How had that happened? Lily was the only reason she was marrying Charles. Wasn't she?

'Of course,' she said, and turned her face toward the beach.

'Jill? One kiss before we go,' he said, and her body quivered in delight.

'Just one?' she whispered, and he chuckled and tugged her close.

Only, of course, happy endings were for fairy-tales. Dreams had a habit of turning into nightmares.

This one did almost the moment they hit the beach. For they were no longer alone.

There were two boys further up the beach. They were tossing stones at seagulls, obviously bored, their body language overtly aggressive.

Showing off to each other. Proving their adolescent macho stuff.

'Hey, there's two from the cripple camp,' one yelled.

They'd be from the resort, Jill thought warily. It was the one problem that Charles hadn't yet been able to solve. The tip of the northern island was home to a resort that was unaffordable to normal people. That meant most guests wanted privacy, but occasionally the super-rich brought their families. This island may be a fabulous eco-resort, famed throughout the world, but indulged adolescents found it boring.

These two looked like trouble. Left to her own devices, Jill would have left the beach fast, pre-empting problems.

But Charles's crutches were up the beach a little, just out of reach of the waves. It'd take him time to reach them.

She ran out of the shallows and grabbed them, then took his arm as he staggered upright. He didn't like it.

'I can manage,' he growled.

'I know you can. But I don't like the look of these two.'

'Zach and Dom Harris,' Charles said, steadying himself as the boys approached. 'I've met them. Their father's Cray Harris, a trucking magnate. They upset one of our kids yesterday. Stella. She's lost a leg from cancer. I wouldn't mind…'

'Confronting them? Please, don't.'

'You don't like a fight?'

'No!'

'I guess you've had enough of that to last a lifetime.' He shrugged and started up the beach. It was a struggle, even for a man of Charles's strength. The sand here was soft and drifted into piles that shifted under his crutches.

'Hey, it must be catching,' one of the boys sneered, edging closer. 'Bloody cripple. I'm going to tell my dad to get us off this place. There's cripples everywhere.'

'I need to have a word with your father myself,' Charles said grimly.

'Yeah, well, he wouldn't want to talk to you,' the oldest of the boys jeered. 'He might catch something.'

Charles closed his eyes. Jill put her hand on his arm, urgent. Don't react, was her silent message. Sticks and stones…

'That's right, hold him up,' the smaller kid yelled.

'He doesn't need holding up,' Jill retorted.

'Maybe you're holding each other up,' the bigger kid yelled. 'What's wrong with you? You got cancer or something?' He was walking closer now, holding something in his hand. It was a sand bomb, Jill saw. A round, hard ball of packed sand, about as big as a baseball.

'Ancient cripples,' the younger boy yelled, and laughed as if he'd said something uproariously funny. 'Put your shirt on, you ugly cow. You're too old for a bikini.'

Ugly cow. The name hit her like a physical blow. She wasn't Jill again. She was a sixteen-year-old kid, losing her baby, losing everything she cared about.

For one awful moment she thought she might be sick.

'Leave it, Charles,' Jill said urgently, as she felt him stiffen in fury. 'Let's get off the beach.'

But he'd stopped. He was facing them square on.

'Do you know how much your words can hurt?'

It was supposed to defuse the situation. It was supposed to be calmness in the face of rage.

But these two didn't want calm. They were out for trouble. If Jill and Charles had tried to keep going up the beach, they would have followed them all the way, taunting them as they went.

Charles had stopped that by facing them. They eyed him uncertainly.

'Cripple,' the younger one said again, as if he was trying to get the older one's approval.

'Don't,' Jill said savagely before she could stop herself, and it was enough. The older boy's face creased into an expression of pure vitriol.

'Don't tell us what we can and can't do, you stupid cow,' he yelled. 'You get off the beach with your crippled boyfriend and take this for good measure.' And before either of them could react he'd lobbed the sandbomb straight at her.

It wasn't just sand. It had a stone in its centre. It hit her hard on the cheek, so hard she staggered back. She would have fallen but Charles's hand came out and gripped her. Hard. One of his crutches fell uselessly to his side but he didn't need it. He hauled her against him and held her.

'Jill…'

She had her hand to her cheek. She could feel a faint warm trickle.

'Jill!'

'I… It's OK.' This was minor. She was used to it.

'Hell!' He turned her to him. 'Hell!' He turned savagely toward the boys.

But the boys had scared themselves. One glance at the blood oozing down Jill's face had them running up the beach like the hounds of hell were after them.

'It was just a stone,' Jill said, but Charles was pushing her hands away, checking for himself.

'Little—'

'Don't.'

'If I could…'

'You can't,' she said flatly. 'And neither can I.'

'What do you mean?' he demanded.

'I mean leave it.'

'We don't have to.'

'I thought you'd have accepted that long ago,' she whispered.

'Being a victim?'

'I…' She faltered. Her face hurt. Her lovely morning was smashed.

She felt about a hundred years old.

'Look, this is OK,' she whispered. 'I just need a sticking plaster and we need to get back to Lily. Beth will be waiting.'

'Jill, we don't have to take this.'

'So what would you have us do? Run after them? I don't think so.' She shook her head, stepped back from his hold and retrieved his crutch from where it had fallen. 'No. Lily's waiting. Thank you…thank you for wanting to…' She shook her head. 'No. We need to not want. I learned that a long time ago.'

CHAPTER EIGHT

THEY returned to the bungalow in silence. Garf met them just off the beach. He greeted them with joy, pushing his great body between them and acting as a goofy buffer.

The big dog was normally a comfort but not now. Jill felt sick.

Charles had withdrawn. He hated it that he hadn't been able to defend her, she thought, but, then, that was what she wanted. She didn't want anyone to fight on her behalf.

No fighting. Ever.

Her cheek stung, but worse was the aftertaste of the aggression she'd seen in those kids.

This was minor compared to what had happened to her in the past. She glanced over at Charles and saw his face was set and stern. And angry.

Angry at her?

Maybe he was, she thought.

She wanted him to be passive.

'I won't do it,' he said as they reached the ramp up to the bungalow, and she stared.

'What?'

'You know damned well,' he growled. '*You* expect me to play the invalid…'

'I don't expect anything.'

'Then start expecting,' he snapped. 'Don't you dare keep playing the victim.'

'I'm not—'

'Let's get off the beach,' he mimicked, and it was so much like her voice that she winced.

'Charles, I only wanted—'

'To run away.'

'What's wrong with that? We can't—'

'We can,' he snapped back at her again.

'Charles? Is that you?' The screen door swung open above them. Beth was standing in the doorway, looking worried.

'Lily,' Charles and Jill said together.

'I can't wake her,' Beth said. 'She's having a nightmare.'

Charles reached her first. Lily was thrashing round on the bed, incoherent.

'Lily,' he said peremptorily, and she stared blindly up at him.

'They're here,' she whimpered. 'They're here. Everywhere.'

'What are, sweetheart?' He leaned forward and lifted her onto his knees. 'What's here?'

'The birds,' she whimpered. 'Daddy, don't let them near. Daddy, the birds…'

It was too much. For Jill, crouching before him, gazing up into his face, she saw the point where things broke.

The events of this night were too much. His rigid control was crumbling.

He'd called Lily sweetheart. He never did. He didn't approve of nicknames. Frivolity.

Lily had called him Daddy.

Lily was delirious.

It didn't matter. The emotions the word had engendered couldn't have been stronger if Lily had been in full control of her senses.

He was fighting back tears.

'I've been sponging her,' Beth said. 'It's not working. I can't get her cool. Charles, we need to admit her.'

'To do what?' Jill whispered, but she already knew the answer.

'This isn't a cold,' Beth said. 'We need to get some fluids on board, we need to get that temperature down and we need to rule out meningitis.'

Meningitis... The word was enough to make her world stop. She tried frantically to think. 'But meningitis... We need a lumbar puncture... We need a paediatrician...'

'We have a paediatric neurosurgeon here on the island,' Beth said. 'Alex Vavunis. His daughter's one of our camp kids. He'll help, I know. If you agree, I'll set it up now. Can I phone for a buggy?'

'Of course,' Jill whispered. She couldn't take her eyes off Lily. The little girl was still struggling with her nightmare. Charles was holding her against him, trying to calm the worst of her struggles.

Lily. Her daughter.

'What are we waiting for?' Charles asked abruptly. 'Beth, make that phone call and see if you can find Alex. Tell him half my kingdom if he'll help. All. Jill, get dressed. Put some antibiotic cream on that face, though. I don't want it being infected.'

'What happened to your face?' Beth asked.

'My face doesn't matter,' Jill whispered. 'Oh, Lily...'

Beth left to make preparations for Lily's admission. Charles held Lily while Jill dressed and stuck a plaster over her cheek, then Jill held Lily while Charles dressed. The buggy arrived before they were ready. The driver was Walter Grubb, hospital handyman. Walter and Dora were permanently based in Crocodile Creek but they'd been desperate to be come over for the opening.

Walter looked just plain desperate now. Charles rolled down the ramp with Lily in his arms. Walter stared down into her white little face and his own face lost colour.

'Oh, no,' he whispered. 'Not Lily. Not our Lil.'

'She's going to be fine,' Jill said strongly, trying to make herself believe it.

'Get in, Jill, and I'll lift her up to you,' Charles said. 'Get out, Garf.'

She hadn't even noticed the dog was in the buggy. Of course. Where there was a buggy, there was Garf.

They didn't need him now.

But Lily had other ideas. She opened her eyes and a trace of normality edged back.

'Garf,' she said and smiled, and that was that. Jill sat in the back of the buggy with Lily in her arms. She wouldn't let Garf lie on top of her as he clearly intended—she needed to keep Lily cool—but Garf took up half the seat.

Charles brought up the rear in his wheelchair, clearly unhappy the buggy wouldn't go as fast as his chair would.

They were an oddly assorted family.

But they were family, Jill thought. Any way she could make them.

Marcia, the clinic nurse, met them at the entrance, pushing a trolley. 'I'll carry her in,' Jill said, but Marcia simply lifted Lily from her arms and laid her on the cool sheets and pillows.

'You can hold her hand,' she said. 'But Beth says we need her cool and you holding her won't help that. Dr Wetherby, Jill, you guys are the parents from this point on. Beth says.'

Jill cast a helpless glance back at Charles. He nodded grimly and Marcia pushed the trolley forward.

There was a medical team waiting for them. Beth and this new doctor Jill hadn't yet met. But Charles obviously had.

'Vavunis,' he said, in a strange, grim voice Jill had never heard before. 'Jill, this is Alex Vavunis. It's good of you to do this for us.'

'I wish I could say it was a pleasure,' the man said. 'I'm just glad I was here.'

'He was here looking for Susie,' Beth said, with an attempt at lightness, and Jill looked sharply up at the big Greek doctor and thought of Susie, their resident physiotherapist. Here we go again, she thought. Crocodile Creek romance. For every-one but Charles and herself?

Marriage and children.

Oh, Lily, please…

She wanted to help. She wanted to be doing what Marcia was doing, helping Beth with equipment, taking obs. She glanced at Charles and saw the same rigid tension in him.

'Can you hear me, Lily?' Alex asked.

'No,' Lily whispered, and they all smiled. But not very much.

Alex had his fingers on her carotid artery, feeling her pulse. He lifted her eyelids, checking pupil reaction. She didn't protest. She seemed almost drugged. Lethargic and uninte-rested. The total opposite to their normally livewire Lily.

'You've got a bug, Lily, is that it?' Alex asked, and Jill's almost unbearable tension levels eased a notch. Alex was using the same tone Charles used when he coped with sick or injured children.

There was no one more competent in a crisis than Charles. It was inappropriate—dangerous even—to treat a child when your emotions were severely compromised, but if Charles couldn't be in charge she was glad this man was here to take his place.

'You've certainly done the right thing admitting her,' Alex said, and the terror washed back threefold.

'Not…? We're not overreacting?'

'Not,' he said bluntly. He was testing Lily's reflexes now, tapping her knees, watching her reactions. The little girl's eyes were closed, as if the light hurt. Alex put down his hammer, but kept Lily's leg bent at the hip, supported by his arm. 'Can you straighten your leg for me, Lily?'

She could. She did. Jill felt her breath rush out in a tiny sob of relief. This was a negative Kernig's sign, one of the major pointers for meningitis.

'She started showing these symptoms yesterday, is that right?' Alex asked them.

'Yes.' The word was almost a growl from Charles. He was

staring fixedly at Lily, as if concentration alone could make her better. 'But it looked like any run-of-the-mill viral illness. She was a bit sniffy. That's all.'

He sounded defensive. For a moment Jill wanted to go to him, hug him, but his body language said not to. His face was set like stone. Expecting the worst?

So was she. She couldn't help him.

'Beth says she was having nightmares.'

'More like hallucinations,' Jill whispered.

'It was a nightmare,' Charles snapped. It seemed that for Charles it was important to get the distinction right. 'I told you, she was upset by the dead bird she found the other day.'

'But she saw it flying around the room,' she whispered.

'She's running a temperature,' Charles replied. 'She's in a strange place.'

They were arguing, Jill thought dully. Why? She couldn't figure it out. She could only figure out that the fingers under hers were hot to the touch. That this was Lily. *Lily*.

As if thinking her name had brought her back to them, Lily opened her eyes. She looked up at Jill, and then over to Charles, and her bottom lip trembled. 'I want to go home.'

Jill was trying hard not to cry. She was being useless, she thought savagely. She was just like any other distraught parent.

She glanced across at Charles and saw he was feeling exactly the same. The urge to go to him…to hold him…was almost overwhelming. But Lily was gripping her hand tightly, and Alex was trying to get her to listen.

'We've got you here so we can take extra-special care of you,' he said. 'Do you remember my name, Lily?'

She shook her head, but barely, however. She was drifting toward sleep, Jill thought, and then, more terrifying, she thought, She's drifting toward unconsciousness.

'How's your neck, poppet?' Alex's voice was insistent. He slipped his hands behind Lily's head. 'In here.'

'It hurts.'

'It's just her glands,' Charles said sharply, but Alex looked over at him and shook his head.

'Let's not take that as read.' He straightened. 'Let's step outside so Lily can go back to sleep. Marcia, can you stay with Lily, please? She could have that dose of paracetamol now.'

They left. It nearly killed Jill to release Lily's hand, but Lily was drifting toward oblivion. She didn't protest as Jill disentangled herself, and if decisions were to be made about what happened now, Jill wanted to hear.

Charles would do her listening, she thought. She trusted Charles. But…this was her daughter.

She walked blindly toward the door. Charles reached it before she did. She put out a hand toward him. Hoping… hoping what? She didn't know. It was a dumb gesture that achieved nothing.

He didn't even acknowledge it, just wheeled through and waited for Alex to start talking.

'Beth's right,' Alex said without preamble. He seemed to know already that neither she nor Charles would tolerate platitudes. 'On the positive side we've got no rash and a negative Kernig's sign, but we can't rule out meningitis without a lumbar puncture.'

Jill closed her eyes. This was the worst of all nightmares.

'I'll do it,' Charles said, and her eyes flew wide. What was he saying? But the strain behind his eyes… He was as terrified as she was.

'No.' Beth's tone was gentle but firm. 'You can't. You know you can't. You have one of the country's top paediatric neurosurgeons right here. How many lumbar punctures have you done on children, Alex?'

'I can't say. A lot.'

'I'd be guessing it's a lot more than Charles or I have done,' Beth said. 'I'm sorry, but it's a no-brainer. You're her daddy, Charles. You get to hold her hand.'

'I'm staying with her,' Jill said, suddenly terrified she'd be left out.

They'd both be with her. They had to be a family. They were all Lily had.

Lily was all they had. She stared down into Charles's frozen face and thought that without Lily they didn't even have each other.

She'd helped with this procedure a hundred times or more in the course of her career. She always hated it.

She hated it so much now she felt sick.

They needed enough staff to position Lily correctly if she struggled. Susie, the physiotherapist, was in the corridor, the first person to hand, and she was appalled to find out why she was needed.

'Not our Lily,' she whispered, hugging Jill.

'Don't worry,' Alex said gently. 'Let's assume this is a needless test, taken to be on the safe side. I'll use plenty of local anaesthetic and make it virtually painless. With so many people around who know and love her, she'll be just fine.'

Dammit, he should be doing the test himself. He should have organised it last night. He should have…

Been of more use.

He felt like lifting the surgical tray and hurling it against the far wall. Instead, all he could do was watch as Alex did what he should be doing.

He did it in his head. He was watching every move of Alex's fingers, as jealous as hell. Helpless. Sick.

'What gauge needle have you got there, Beth?' Alex was asking.

'A twenty.'

'Does the stylet fit the barrel?'

'All checked. We're good.'

'Right. Lily, let's get you lying on your side, sweetheart.

We're going to do a test on your back that'll help us find out what's the matter with you. It'll tell us which medicine is right for you. OK?'

'O-OK,' Lily whispered but it clearly wasn't. Dammit, he was close to tears, Charles thought.

'Jill, you stay close to her head and hold her hand. Charles, can you keep a hand on Lily's hip and legs? Marcia? Legs for you, too, and, Susie, I'll get you beside me with extra support for Lily's chest and arms.'

Alex was OK, Charles thought. He was ensuring Lily would stay still. He knew what he was doing.

It didn't make him feel any better.

Beth was swabbing Lily's lower back with antiseptic and Alex pressed along the spine, counting carefully, looking for the space between the third and fourth vertebrae. He was talking but Charles wasn't hearing. If he could go through this himself in Lily's stead…

He glanced along at Jill and he knew she was feeling exactly the same.

His feeling of helplessness intensified. What sort of parent was he? What sort of husband?

There was still a smear of blood on Jill's cheek, running down from her sticking plaster. The sight of it made him feel even worse.

'Small scratch,' Alex warned Lily, and Charles felt Lily stiffen in terror. She whimpered at the feel of the needle. Jill, too. It was a tiny sound, almost inaudible, but he heard it nonetheless.

'Talk to her, Jill,' he said urgently, and Jill cast him a frightened glance. He met her eyes with a silent, strong message. Children sensed fear.

She swallowed. He saw her take two, three deep breaths, and then crouch and whisper to Lily. He couldn't hear what she was saying.

He wanted to hear. But he needed to watch Alex.

There was no faulting Alex. It was a textbook procedure, skilfully executed. But still Charles watched every single move.

Angling the needle with care, Alex moved slowly and surely, withdrawing the stylet often to check for the drip of any cerebrospinal fluid. The decrease in the resistance to the needle would mean he'd know precisely when he was in the right place. And in seconds he was. Clear fluid dripped easily, and Beth had the required tubes ready. The stylet was replaced, the system withdrawn and a sterile swab pressed to the puncture site.

Charles hadn't been aware that he'd stopped breathing. But maybe it was just as well he was sitting down. He couldn't have done this for Lily, he acknowledged. He felt sick.

'All over,' Alex said into the stillness. 'You were a very brave girl, Lily. Well done.'

Charles wasn't sure she could hear. Jill was nose to nose with her, still whispering. There it was again, that stab of jealousy. He wanted it. He wanted this closeness.

He was useless.

'What about blood tests?' he demanded, trying to get his mind back into gear.

'Let's get an IV line in and collect the bloods at the same time.'

'Antibiotic of choice?' This was Beth's job, asking these questions, he thought, but he couldn't help himself. And everyone seemed to understand his need.

'Benzylpenicilin IV,' Alex said, talking to Beth as well as to Charles. 'She's going to need half-hourly neurological checks. Responses to light and verbal commands, hand grip on both sides—Beth, you know the drill. Fluid restriction for the moment as well until we get a better idea of what we're dealing with.'

'We'll get the samples away on the first ferry or flight,' Beth said.

'Mike can take them now,' Charles snapped, and then, as

everyone looked at him he gave a shame-faced grin, he added, 'I know. But this is my kid. I help fund the service; it cares for my kid.'

Beth smiled at him, her smile saying she understood. 'That's great. It'll mean we should get the first results back later today.'

She hesitated, looking from Charles to Jill and back again, as if trying to think of something she could say to reassure them. 'It's so good you're both here with Lily,' she said softly. 'Poor little Robbie Henderson's come in with a bug, and his mother's a single mum. There's no way she can leave four other children to be here.'

'What's wrong with Robbie?' Lily whispered. Now the adults around her had started to relax she seemed to have stirred a little. 'Is he sick, like me?'

'Kind of,' Beth said, and glanced toward her friend. 'Susie, you know Robbie? Is he one of your patients?'

'Robbie? Ten years old. Cerebral palsy?'

'That's him.'

'I do know him. There were no requests for any special programme for him. He did join in with my swimming-pool group once but camp activities have been enough to keep his joints mobile. Has he got flu?'

'He started vomiting in the night. He's running a temperature and complaining of a headache and sore eyes.'

'I've got sore eyes,' Lily whispered, 'but I haven't vomited.'

Jill was so glad it was over. So relieved she felt dizzy. Now all she wanted was the results. She was with Charles every inch of the way. If all fast results required was money, she'd have mortgaged her soul.

She glanced up at Charles but he was frowning, staring at Beth with a pucker between his brows that he always had when he was worried.

He was distracted, Jill thought. Worried about something else? About Robbie? 'I'll see you later, Lily,' he told her. 'I've got to go and get things ready for our big opening this afternoon. Jill's going to stay with you, aren't you, Jill?'

'Of course.'

He nodded abruptly and Jill knew for sure then that he was worried about something else. This mind reading worked both ways, she thought. But he wasn't sharing.

'Maybe it's the same thing,' Alex said thoughtfully. 'You want me to take a look?'

'If he gets any worse, yes, please,' Beth said gratefully.

'If you have an influenza virus doing the rounds it's not that uncommon to get meningoencephalitis. It should be self-limiting and only require supportive measures.'

'But I want to know straight away if we have any more cases,' Charles said. 'There's been a couple of staff off colour over the last two days. If there's a flu bug—'

'The last thing we want is for it to spread to our sick kids,' Beth finished for him.

Charles nodded. He wheeled over to Lily's bed and took her hand. Leaning over, he kissed her lightly on the forehead. So much for barrier nursing, Jill thought.

'I love you, sweetheart,' Charles whispered, and Jill blinked.

So much for any barriers at all.

'I need to go,' he told her, and wheeled away. Without saying goodbye to her.

OK. There were definitely still some barriers.

It was the longest day of her life.

All day Jill sat by Lily's bed, watching her little girl grow sicker. Maybe they should ring her uncle, she thought. She mentioned it to Charles mid-morning. Charles made the phone call and came back, grim-faced.

'He says kids get sick all the time. If we're going to adopt her, get used to worrying.'

'He doesn't care,' Jill whispered.

'We're her parents,' Charles said.

He couldn't be with them all the time. There were urgent pressures outside. The gala dinner was taking place tonight over at the resort. Major sponsors had contributed megabucks. They were expecting to be thanked in style, and not just in the short few moments of speechmaking tonight.

He was trying to keep the worst of the pressure away from her, Jill thought. He wheeled through into Lily's ward every half-hour or so and she saw the effort it cost him to stop the wheels spinning, to slow as he entered the room, to pause by Lily's bedside and be still.

The official opening—the ribbon cutting—was at four. She didn't leave Lily. Charles came in soon after, looking grey.

'Can't someone else take over out there?' she asked him.

'I've talked half these people into contributing,' he said grimly. 'I've twisted arms, I've hauled in favours; in some cases it's pretty much close to blackmail. If I don't keep thanking people—if I'm not at the official dinner tonight—there's no saying that some of that money won't be forthcoming. We've promised this island to too many kids…'

'It's a wonderful thing…'

'Yeah,' he said bitterly. 'It's so damned important that I have to go dress up in a penguin suit.'

'It is important,' she said solidly. 'I'll be with Lily every minute.'

But she wanted to be with him. The strain on his face was well nigh unbearable. All these people surrounding him tonight…they wouldn't know Charles's daughter was ill. Even if Alex told them what was happening, well, Lily was just his adoptive daughter after all, and not really even that yet.

They wouldn't know how much he cared.

He was looking down into Lily's face now. She was drifting in and out of sleep, feverish, fretful.

'We've done everything we can,' he said. 'We've hit her with everything we can. She wouldn't get better treatment if we evacuated her to the Children's Hospital.'

'She'd be worse,' Jill said stolidly. 'There'd be the flight, the strangeness. Here she knows every single member of the medical team apart from Alex, and she's already starting to recognise him.'

'He's good, isn't he?' Charles said, momentarily diverted.

'He's been in twice again, just to check.'

'Good of him.' He stared down at Lily's pallid face and a muscle pulled at the corner of his mouth. 'You'll buzz me the minute she gets worse.'

'She won't get worse.'

'She might before she pulls the corner,' he warned. 'Twelve hours before the antibiotic takes hold.'

'That's if she has meningitis. There's still no rash.'

'The test results should be back soon.' He glanced at his watch. 'Hell. I have to go. I need to—'

'What else is wrong?'

He stilled. 'What do you mean, what else is wrong?'

'I know you, Charles,' she said softly. 'Yes, you're worried about Lily, but you're worried about something else.'

'We have three sick kids now. And a couple of adults. Isn't that enough to worry about?'

'So it's flu?' She said it almost eagerly.

'I'm thinking yes.'

'But what?' she said, still watching his face.

'Nothing.'

'I know your face,' she said. 'This is something bad. What's wrong with them all getting flu? We could relax if it's just flu.'

'Not if it's bird flu,' he said heavily.

CHAPTER NINE

FOR a moment she couldn't take it in. She stared at him in disbelief, and then, involuntarily, she turned back to Lily.

Lily's eyes were closed. There were dark smudges under them, her pale little face looking almost bleached. The fingers tucked into Jill's hand were hot and dry.

Bird flu. The deadly flu virus that had the world terrified.

'She picked up the bird on the beach,' Charles said heavily. 'I've been going over and over it in my head. There are dead birds all over the island. The shearwaters arrive here as part of their regular migratory pattern—they come to breed. But this year they seem to be coming to die, and there's confirmed cases of bird flu just north of us.' Then, at the look on her face, he swore. 'Hell, Jill, I didn't want to scare you with this. I didn't want to tell anyone. But I'm going nuts.'

Was it then? Afterwards she thought maybe it was. She'd been so caught up with Lily—she still was—she was terrified for her small daughter. But in that instant something changed.

Up until then Charles had seemed aloof, distant, even hero material. She'd admired him enormously. She'd watched as he'd fought to build this medical service so it was second to none. She'd been in awe of him.

But now…he seemed lost. This threat alone he could cope with, she thought, but he kept looking at Lily. He wanted all his attention to be on Lily.

Even this morning…she'd been hit and he hadn't been able to prevent it. His control was shattered.

He needed her, she thought with a flash of insight that was almost overwhelming. He needed her right now almost as much as Lily did.

Lily was asleep. Her priority right now had to be Charles. She carefully disentangled herself from Lily and pushed her chair round so she could take both Charles's hands in hers.

'Birds die,' she said softly. 'Come on, Charles. Every time I'm on a beach I see a decomposing bird or two. It's nature. When birds die we don't have undertakers coming round to put them in mahogany coffins. Who's to say there wasn't a bit of a baby-boomer swell in numbers, say, five years ago— how long do birds live? And now there's a vast geriatric population creaking their way back to the island to die?'

He smiled but his smile didn't reach his eyes. 'There's far more dead birds than usual. I've been talking to the rangers. They're worried, too.'

'So this afternoon…'

'I've been on the internet. The strain of avian bird flu that's been threatening the countries north of here is called H5N1. The symptoms match Lily. And Robbie. And…'

'And any other flu,' she said stoutly. Then her voice faltered a little. 'But it doesn't react to treatment…'

'She's holding her own, Jill.'

'Do you really think…?'

'I can't be sure,' he said, tugging his hands away so he could rake his hair. 'I'm ordering blood tests. I've been onto a couple of epidemiologists from the mainland. The symptoms are non-specific. A lot depends on whether Lily's meningitis test comes back positive.'

'So we're hoping for meningitis?'

'No! Hell, Jill, I don't know what I want. Look, I shouldn't be saying this even to you. There's only a tiny chance I'm right. But if I am…I need to have everything in place. No one's leaving the island tonight. We've got priority on all blood testing. A decision will be made in the morning.'

'To close the island down?'

Marcia came in then, to check Lily's drip. They stopped talking and Marcia saw the look of strain on both their faces and felt the need to stay and chat and reassure them.

Jill was screaming inwardly for her to leave. Charles was glancing at his watch. There were so many pressures…

That he'd shared this with her was huge, she thought. Whether he wanted it or not, she reached out and took his hand again. And held it. He stared down at their linked hands as if he wasn't quite sure how to respond.

'You're thinking quarantine?' she said as Marcia buzzed out again, and he nodded.

'Yes.'

'Is there vaccination?'

'I'm organising it now. Provisionally. There's no flu vaccine specific to H5N1 but there are antivirals we can give that make it much less leth—harmful.'

'It is lethal,' she whispered, turning back to Lily.

'From what I've read, if this was a bad case Lily would be even sicker than she is now,' he told her. 'She's a strong little girl. She has the best possible care.'

'We have to keep her,' she whispered.

'We will.' He lifted her ring finger, and his mouth twisted into a crooked smile. 'Our engagement's still on, then?'

'Of course.'

'I'm no catch.'

'You are,' she said solidly, and her grip on his hands tightened. 'Look at you. You've got everyone on this island wanting a piece of you right now. You're worried sick about Lily. You're worried sick about bird flu. Have you told anyone else on the island?'

'No.'

'Because you don't want panic. You only told me because

I wouldn't let you off the hook. You keep it all to yourself. And tonight…you have this damned dinner…'

'I have to go.'

'You don't. If people there knew the reason—'

'If they knew I wasn't there because I was figuring out how the hell to enforce quarantine, we'd have people trying frantically to get off the island tonight. If they thought I wasn't there because I was desperately worried about Lily then we'd have every one of the Croc Creek staff over here in a bedside vigil. It's bad enough that you won't be there.'

'I can't be,' she whispered.

'Of course you can't,' he told her, and then suddenly he tugged her forward so she was leaning into him. He pushed himself to his feet, pulled her up and against him and hugged her. It was a weird, un-Charles-like gesture. It was a gesture of pure physical comfort, nothing else. He released her, but as they both sank back into their chairs he put his fingers out to touch her face and run them across her cheekbone. Gently pausing at the sticking plaster on her cheek.

'You will look after her for me?'

'Of course I will.' She was feeling choked, close to tears.

'I do need to go.'

'And put your dinner suit on.' She managed a smile. 'You look fabulous in a dinner suit.'

'I need my fiancée beside me,' he said, but she shook her head.

'Of course you don't. You don't need anyone.'

'I wish that was the truth,' he said. 'For your sake…' He grimaced. 'Enough. You will ring me if anything changes.'

'Of course.'

'And what we just talked about…'

'Is nonsense talk,' she said. 'Bird flu. Ridiculous.' But she met his eyes and their gazes held. He really believed it, she thought.

'I know,' she said softly. 'It'd cause major panic. I won't say a word. You go off and strut your tail feathers to all the corporate sponsors and I'll keep the home fires burning.'

'There's a bit of a mixed metaphor there.'

'Probably,' she admitted. 'Mixed is the least of how I'm feeling. But, Charles…'

'Yes?'

'See if you can enjoy yourself, just a bit,' she said. 'This opening…you've worked so hard for it. You deserve this night.'

'Then I'm getting what I deserve,' he said, and his voice was suddenly as grim as death.

The official dinner was a glittering occasion, a who's who of Australian corporate money plus anyone who'd been in on the construction of the kids' camp from the beginning. There were corporate bankers, with their wives wearing designer outfits worth thousands. There were doctors from around the world, and politicians. There were the likes of Dora and Walter Grubb in their Sunday best, rubbing shoulders with wealth and loving every minute of it.

Charles moved through the crowd with care, spending time with whoever needed personal attention to ensure further sponsorship, and also making sure anonymous donors, those who'd come because they wanted to see what their money had achieved rather than make a splash themselves, also got attention. The people who'd donated in a small way, like the Grubbs who'd worked tirelessly for this, had to be thanked as well.

He was good at it now. He could almost do it in his sleep.

He could watch the door at the same time. Harry, chief police officer from Crocodile Creek, was working through what needed to be done if the tests came back inconclusive. They were assuming the worst. Like Charles, Harry was wearing a dinner suit so his coming and going was inconspicuous. The messages he was passing on to Charles weren't good.

Neither were the messages he was getting from Beth. 'Two more cases,' she texted him just before the speeches started, and he felt sick.

Then, just before he was due to speak, he received another text. From Jill.

'Lily's awake. We both send our love. Knock 'em dead, Daddy.'

He stared down at the screen of his cell phone and his rigid self-control almost deserted him.

They were great. Jill and Lily.

They deserved a proper family.

He stood up to deliver his speech, holding the sides of the lectern to steady himself. There were flashlights all around—this camp had the right ingredients to make news all by itself in tomorrow's press. Halfway through his speech he thought, What if it is bird flu? The media will go nuts. It was almost enough to give him pause.

He didn't pause. His rigid self-control held him in good stead. He finished speaking, to thunderous applause. A politician made a longer speech to slightly less applause.

It was over. The formalities were done. The Crocodile Creek Kids' Camp was open.

To be shut tomorrow?

It wasn't a great thought. There were people milling around, congratulating him, wanting to shake his hand. He was starting to seem preoccupied, he thought. 'He's worried about Lily,' he heard Dora say to Grubby.

How soon could he get back to them?

The night dragged on, interminable. He smiled until his face ached. He was back in his wheelchair now, and his left hand stayed in his pocket. He had his phone on vibrate. Willing it to ring? Willing it not to ring. Jill would tell him the minute things changed. He knew she would.

Dammit, he wanted to be there so much he felt sick.

Finally, just when he was about to lose it, tell these people they weren't wanted, to get the hell out of there, Beth appeared at the door. He was talking to Rick Allandale, the father of one of the camp kids. Rick was overbearing and pompous and had been telling him all the things that should be improved in the camp.

Beth slid easily into the conversation, smiled charmingly at Rick and intercepted an elderly man with a vast pot belly.

'Sir Henry… I'm not sure if you know Rick Allendale. Lauren, Rick's daughter, is one of our very favourite camp kids. Rick, Henry is head of Scotsdale Packing. You were saying we needed more recreational facilities? I'm betting if you told Henry exactly what we needed you might both be able to work something out to the benefit of everyone.'

She smiled sweetly at them both, then turned her back on them, effectively getting Charles for herself.

'See,' she said, grinning at the look on his face. 'It's not only you who can play the politician. Want some good news?'

'Yes!'

'The test result's come back clear. No meningitis.'

He closed his eyes. Of all the scenarios, meningitis was the worst. But then…

'And her temp's dropped,' Beth said. 'Not much but enough to think that maybe she's turning the corner. She fell asleep about an hour ago. It seems a lovely, natural sleep.'

So even if it was bird flu, she might recover. The consequences of bird flu would be appalling, but for now all he could think was that Lily was improving.

How could he worry about the greater good when his kid was threatened? It was an impossible ask.

'Do you want to tell Jill it's not meningitis?' Beth asked.

'You haven't told her?'

'Nope. If you go through to the ward now, you'll see why not.'

'I can't leave here.'

'Yes, you can,' she said forcibly. 'If anyone dares question it I'll say Lily's test results have come through negative for meningitis and you need to tell Jill. There's not a soul in this room—even the ghastly Allendales—who'd question that. Go, Charles.'

'But—'

'But you have a dozen or more Croc Creek doctors working this room,' she said. 'You've done your duty here. Your duty now is to your family.'

She sounded so stern that he almost smiled.

'Yes, ma'am,' he said, and he went.

It wasn't just Lily who was sleeping. It was Jill as well.

Barrier nursing? He didn't think so. Jill had slid onto the bed and held her little daughter close. Lily was curled in against her in a pose as old as time itself.

They slept.

Charles wheeled across to the bed and stared down at the pair of them. The tension in Jill's face had eased in sleep. She looked younger, he thought. She looked…vulnerable.

The contrast between the women he'd just been with was stark. This morning Jill had hauled on a T-shirt and shorts. Maybe she'd brushed her hair but it surely hadn't seen a comb for the rest of the day. Her curls were tangled out onto the pillow behind her.

The sticking plaster on her cheek looked almost shocking.

He wheeled to the bottom of the bed and fetched the thermometer. Carefully, so he wouldn't disturb either of them, he slid it into the fold under Lily's arm.

And waited.

Thirty-eight point one.

It was down a point and a half since he'd last been here. It was down half a point since Beth had checked half an hour ago.

He closed his eyes in thankfulness and when he opened them Jill was watching him.

Blankly. Expecting the worst.

'Not bad,' he whispered, and because he couldn't help himself he reached over and touched her nose. It was a feather touch, a simple way of grounding him to her. 'Don't look like that, love. The test results have come back. No meningitis.'

'No?'

'No.'

'And…' She swallowed. 'And bird flu?'

'Those tests will take longer,' he said gravely. 'But Lily's temperature is dropping. Beth thinks, and I concur, that she's coming out of the woods. Even if it is bird flu, she's looking like she'll be OK.'

'Oh, Charles.' She didn't move. She couldn't. She was on her side, facing him, but Lily was curled in against her. A slow tear trickled down her cheek and Charles grabbed his beautifully starched handkerchief from his dinner suit pocket and wiped it away.

Something flashed outside the window. Lightning? He barely caught it and it was gone.

No matter. Jill was choking back a chuckle. 'I don't think those handkerchiefs are meant for real wiping.'

'It's damned useless if it isn't,' he growled. He sighed. 'Jill, I need to go.'

'Of course you do,' she whispered, though her face clouded.

'There are other sick children.'

'Of course.' She took a grip. 'I'm sorry. That was really selfish of me. How did your dinner go?'

'Interminably.'

She smiled. 'Your favourite thing—making speeches.'

'Yeah, well…' He was smiling at her too damned much. He caught himself and tugged the wheels of his chair away from the bed. 'I…I'll see you later.'

'You need to go to bed.'

'Not yet.' He hesitated. 'Will you…?' There was a host of questions in these two little words but Jill didn't feel competent to answer any of them.

'I need to stay here,' she said.

'Of course you do.'

'Not because…'

'I understand that, too,' he assured her, and maybe he did and maybe he didn't. On a logical level he understood. On a gut level he hated it.

'Goodnight, then.'

'Charles?'

'Yes?'

'You're not going to kiss us goodnight?'

He stared at them both. His mouth twisted again, as if there was dark humour in what he was thinking.

'Barrier nursing,' he said at last, and he wheeled away and left the ward.

He'd called her love.

'Don't look like that, love.'

He hadn't even known he'd done it, she thought. It had been an involuntary figure of speech.

He was calling Lily sweetheart. He'd called her love.

It was enough.

There was a long way to go, she thought sleepily. She thought back to Charles's reaction on the beach, his hatred of the fact that he couldn't defend her. There'd always be a barrier, she thought.

It didn't matter. He'd called her love. He'd touched her nose.

She was behaving like a moonstruck teenager.

She didn't care, she thought suddenly, defiantly. She was in bed with her daughter and all the signs were that Lily would recover. The appalling threat of meningitis had been lifted.

Other kids were sick.

They were, and she'd worry about them in the morning. She promised herself that. But for tonight... Tonight she had Lily in her arms and Charles had called her love.

It was enough to be going on with, she thought dreamily.

Lily stirred in her sleep and Jill hugged her closer. Usually Lily pulled away. She didn't much like cuddles.

Not now. She was huddled against Jill like a kitten needing warmth.

Tonight she'd take this as a happy ever after, Jill thought. She'd ignore Charles's comments about barrier nursing. This was time out.

It was a time for believing that love could really work.

CHAPTER TEN

'YOU'VE got to close the island.'

It wasn't what he wanted to hear. He hadn't slept. The bungalow had seemed cold and empty without Jill and Lily. The big bed had seemed…well, too damned big. At dawn he'd come back to the hospital. Lily had been fast asleep and Jill had gone to find a change of clothes and take a shower. And now this…

He'd talked to Beth. He'd talked to the rangers and to Harry, as representative of the state's police force.

Even then he'd been unsure, but Beth had suggested consulting her ex-husband. Angus Stuart was a pathologist with an interest in epidemiology. He'd been over at the resort at the medical conference.

Fifteen minutes after he arrived at the medical centre he was telling Charles what he didn't want to hear.

'You must have had similar thoughts yourself, given the number of dead birds,' Angus told him. 'We have to quarantine the whole island until we know more. It's a thousand to one chance that it's anything sinister, but lower odds than that are still too big a chance to take.'

The implications were enormous. Charles was struggling to take them in.

'It has to be done and it has to be done now,' Angus said in a voice that brooked no opposition. 'It'd be criminal to allow even one person who could be carrying a deadly virus to leave the island. We'll have to get the police and health authorities to trace anyone who's left in the last week and isolate them as well.'

That'd be the easy part, Charles thought. But convincing people to stay…especially if there was a deadly disease around…

'I need to talk to Harry again,' he said heavily. 'There's so much…' He took a deep breath. 'It needs to be me who breaks the news. I'll set up a briefing room. I'll contact Harry.'

He hesitated. 'But first I need to talk to Jill.'

She was just out of the shower. She was sitting in the chair beside Lily's bed, towelling her hair dry. She looked up as he entered and smiled, nodding toward the sleeping Lily, signalling that she was better still. And then her smile faded as he glanced briefly at Lily and returned his gaze directly to her.

'What is it?'

'Nothing more than last night,' he said quickly. Damn, he hadn't meant to panic her. 'But we've decided to close the island.'

'We?'

'Beth's ex-husband is here. He's at the resort, giving a paper at the conference. He's an epidemiologist.'

'He says it's bird flu?' The fear in her eyes was still there. He wheeled forward and took her hands. They were wet from her hair. They felt great, he thought. She had the best hands. Lovely, practical, caring hands. Seductive hands. Spine-tinglingly sensitive hands. A man could fall in love with those hands.

He had a flashback of what those hands had been doing…had it only been the night before last?—and he had to concentrate fiercely on what needed to be said.

'Angus says it's a thousand to one it's not bird flu,' he said. 'But whatever the virus is, it's nasty, aggressive and spreading. Given we have dead birds, given how sick Lily and Robbie grew, and how fast, we have no choice.'

'People will panic,' she whispered.

'They will. I need you not to panic.'

'I won't panic.'

'Thank you,' he said, and went to pull away. But she held on.

'You look exhausted.'

'I'm fine.'

'You're not.'

'You look after you and Lily,' he said. 'I've looked after myself so long now I don't know any other way.'

The hardest part was breaking the news. As many staff as could be spared, from the camp, the clinic, the national park and from the resort, were asked to attend the lecture theatre at the convention centre.

Thank God Angus was here, Charles thought. The man spoke informatively, in a way that was intended not to spread alarm.

'It's highly unlikely to be bird flu,' he told them. 'But because it's similar to a flu virus, we believe flu vaccine might stave off infection in people not already infected. A number of you are hospital staff or in related medical fields so you'll have already had flu shots this year, but we're flying in more stock and will vaccinate everyone on the island who isn't already covered. There are also antivirals which will help ease symptoms. We believe we have things under control. The quarantine is a precaution only and the last thing we need is panic.'

Charles was watching faces. There were resort guests here, too. How had they found about this? Damn, this lecture wasn't meant for them. He'd meant this to be for staff, with tactics worked out here to minimise alarm.

It was too late now. There was definite alarm.

'We should have tests results within forty-eight hours,' Angus was saying. 'That means in forty-eight hours you'll probably all be able to go home. But in the meantime we must act as if bird flu is a possibility, however remote. We know that more than ninety-nine per cent of bird flu cases have come from direct contact with infected birds, so it's imperative we warn guests and staff to keep away from all birds, whether alive or dead. We've already ordered full body suits with rebreathing masks to be flown to the island. As soon as they arrive we'll roster people to collect and dispose of any remaining dead birds.'

He didn't say the cull might end up including all birds, Charles thought bleakly. The bird life on Wallaby Island was fantastic. A cull was unthinkable.

It had to be thought of.

There were questions coming at them from all sides now. He had to concentrate as he and Angus fielded question after desperate question. Then, just as he thought the questions were at an end, there was a stir at the back of the room. A thick-set man and his two sons. Cray Harris, Zach and Dom.

The two thugs from the beach yesterday, with their father.

Almost the moment he saw them he saw Jill. She'd come in late, and was standing at the back, almost hidden in the crush.

Why had she come? To support him? The thought was a shot of warmth in an atmosphere of chill fear.

'You can't stop us leaving,' Cray Harris was saying—shouting.

'We can.' It was Harry, dressed in his official police uniform. He'd been standing quietly to one side, not wanting to make this seem any greater a threat than it already was.

His words caused a deathly silence.

'How?' the man said belligerently.

'Quarantine rules granted to me by the Department of Health mean I have jurisdiction to arrest anyone trying to leave the island,' Harry said, strolling to the front of the small stage and meeting Cray's belligerence head on. 'Angus and Charles here have been telling me that this quarantine is likely to be short—probably only for two days. Chances are this isn't bird flu. We're probably overreacting.

When the testing comes through negative everyone will be allowed to leave—except for those people who've attempted to break quarantine regulations. Those people will find themselves in jail for the two years' maximum sentence the law allows. You try and leave the island, I'll lock you up. As simple as that.'

It put things in perspective. There were people who'd been clearly about to ask the same question. Charles had seen the beginnings of plans forming—private boats, a bribe in exchange for a blind eye.

Harry's statement stopped that in its tracks.

'We'll keep you informed every step of the way,' Harry assured everyone. 'Thank you. But, Mr Harris, can I ask you to stay behind? I need to talk to you and to your sons.'

That was the end of the briefing. Their audience filed out, muttering among themselves in subdued tones. Jill looked as if she might leave, too, but Charles beckoned her down to his side.

'I need to get back to Lily,' she said as she reached him. She felt odd here. She'd only come because, well, because Lily was asleep and it seemed right to be here. Charles shouldn't have to bear everything on his broad shoulders.

'Yes, but you need to hear this,' he said. 'Harry was thinking he'd do this later, but we're all together now.'

'What?' She gazed around, puzzled. Everyone was gone barring Charles, Harry and Cray Harris, and Zach and Dom, standing uncertainly at the top of the tiered seating.

'Come on down,' Harry said cordially.

'Why the hell?' The man looked furious.

'I need to explain why I'm not planning to arrest your sons,' Harry said.

There was a sharp intake of breath. Cray swung round to face his boys. 'What the—'

'Come down,' Harry said again, his voice turning steely.

'We're going back to the hotel,' Zach muttered, but his

father put a large hand in the small of his son's back and propelled him down the steps with force.

'Thank you,' Harry said, but he didn't smile.

'What the hell's going on? I've got things to do,' Cray said angrily. 'I've a hundred phone calls to make.'

'And so do your boys have things to do,' Harry said gently. 'Boys, this is Sister Jill Shaw, our director of nursing. Do you recognise her?'

'She's the… She was swimming yesterday,' Zach muttered, not looking at her.

'Charles tells me you threw a stone at her. You cut her face.' Harry's voice had changed completely now. His tone was almost frightening. It was so soft they could hardly hear it, but for Jill, who'd had no idea what had been coming, it sent a shiver down her spine.

'We didn't,' Zach spat, but his face said he had.

'You know, both Charles and Jill say you did,' Harry said. 'And one of our groundsmen, Walter Grubb, saw you as well. They all say you threw the stone, deliberately intending to hurt her.'

'It was an accident,' Zach muttered.

'Then I'm sure you want to make up for it.'

Jill's gaze flew to Charles. This was his doing, she thought. How had he managed…?

'We have protective suits arriving here in two hours,' Harry went on. 'Then we'll be asking for volunteers to spread out over the island and collect bird carcasses. I expect you two to be our first volunteers.'

The boys gasped as one. It wasn't a prospect that would attract anyone. For these two, the indulged sons of a very rich man, it must seem unthinkable.

It was unthinkable. 'In your dreams,' Dom jeered.

'Then I have no choice but to arrest you for the assault on Sister Jill Shaw,' Harry said implacably. 'You do not have to say anything but anything you do say—'

'Hey,' Cray said, and held up his hand. 'Hang on there!'

'Yes, Mr Harris?'

'You guys threw stones at a nurse?' he demanded incredulously of his sons.

'We didn't know she was a nurse,' Zach whined. 'I mean, she was with a cripple.'

The big man stared at his sons, truly appalled. 'You guys threw stones? To hurt someone? Why the hell?'

'We were bored.'

There was a moment's stunned silence.

'I'll give you bored,' Cray roared, embarrassed, humiliated, close to apoplectic with fury. 'Of all the stupid, dumb, mindless… Right. That's it. Your mother's indulgence stops now. As does mine. To think I let you out of school for this holiday… First you can apologise. Right here. Right now. If there's anything else Sister Shaw wants you to do, you'll do that, too. And then, of course, you're volunteering. You're volunteering until this bird thing clears,' he said furiously. 'Even if it takes a year.'

They were left alone.

Jill felt…winded.

'You set that up,' she said at last, wonderingly. 'With all you had on your mind, you set that up.'

'If you thought I'd have let those little thugs get away with it…'

'You're still angry about it?'

'Of course I'm angry.' Charles looked at her steadily. 'You would have liked it if I'd have been able to chase them and knock their heads together?'

'I would have liked it if I'd have been able to chase them and knock their heads together.'

'But you never would. Pacifist Jill.'

'Is there something wrong with that?'

'Not if it's what you want,' he said, and she flushed.

'Of course I want it.'

'Which is why it's OK to marry me,' he said softly. 'You don't think I'm capable of violence.'

'I didn't say that.'

'You didn't have to.' He said it bleakly but then caught himself and smiled. 'I'm sorry. It's unfair. We are what we are. Damaged goods.'

'Hey, speak for yourself.' She tried to smile back but her smile didn't reach her eyes.

'That's how you see yourself.'

'Look, there's nothing wrong with not wanting violence,' she retorted.

'Of course there's not. But you're frightened of it. Not normally frightened. You're expecting it. All the time. You see it as the norm.'

'I don't.'

'Do you see marriage to me as safe?'

'I don't see any marriage as safe,' she confessed, and then pushed her hair wearily back from her face. 'I'm sorry. Charles, we can make a go of this. We can have fun.'

'When you forget that you're frightened.' He looked at her steadily. 'You're still terrified of Kelvin. But you're not frightened of bird flu. You slept all night with Lily. When you need to be, you're brave.'

'I am, aren't I?' she said mockingly. 'It's only loud voices that turn me to jelly. A little bit of bird flu is nothing.'

'So we need to avoid loud noises.'

'It'd be good,' she whispered. She hesitated. 'I'm sorry. That sounds wimpy. I decided that I don't want to be wimpy. It was only the stone that brought it all back.' And the words. *Ugly cow...*

'Damn.' He swore harshly into the stillness and pushed himself to his feet. He'd braked his chair so he could use it to steady himself but he didn't hold it. Instead, he reached out and took Jill's hands, drawing her into him. 'If I was—'

'Don't,' she muttered, distressed. 'There's too many ifs.'

'There are, aren't there?' he said ruefully, stroking her hair. 'If we could turn back time… But we can't. What we can do is make this as good as it gets.'

'That's a movie,' she whispered. 'As good as it gets.'

'Did they live happily ever after?'

'Probably not,' she admitted. 'But better than apart.'

'That's what this will be for you?'

'I… Maybe.'

'Jill, sex with you…'

'It was good, wasn't it?' she whispered, and the smile came back into her voice.

'As good as it gets?' he said. 'Or better?'

'Maybe we need to work on it,' she suggested, and she tried to keep her voice prim but failed.

He held her at arm's length and smiled at her. 'You're laughing.'

'Not me. Sex is a serious business.'

'Really?'

'Maybe not,' she said. 'Maybe that's why people do it in the dark. So they don't have to see that it looks ridiculous. All those wobbly bits.'

'There speaks a true medical professional,' he said, and grinned. 'Wobbly bits. Which particular pieces of our anatomy would you be referring to?'

'You'll never know while the lights are out,' she said, and then thought, Whoa, what had she said? She wasn't asking. She wasn't even suggesting.

But Charles was looking at her with a gleam that said he thought she had been asking, she had been suggesting.

'Tonight?'

'Lily's ill.'

'I'm thinking Lily may well have turned the corner.'

'I won't leave her in the hospital by herself.'

'She'll be fine.'

'She might be fine. I don't want her to be fine without me.'

'It's OK for us to be fine without each other?'

'Of course it is,' she said, startled. 'We don't want dependency.'

'Of course we don't.' But he didn't sound sure.

He'd been stroking her hair, sifting her curls with his long, lean fingers. It did lovely things to her. More than lovely. It was making her feel… Melting.

Was the head supposed to be an erogenous zone? She'd have to look it up. Later. After he'd stopped. There was no way she was stopping him now.

But he stopped himself and she could have wept with loss.

'I need to get back to work,' he said reluctantly. 'We need to get this quarantine sorted. The powers that be are sending in a biohazard lab we need to set up. There's a million protocols. I need to get antiviral therapy started.'

'Plus you'll have hysterical people wanting to get off the island.'

'That's Harry's job,' he said seriously. 'He's the policeman. He copes with the scary stuff.'

'You just cope with the deadly disease.'

'*We* do,' he said. 'Jill, I can't tell you how much it means to me that you're here.'

But his voice was formal again. What was it? she wondered. What had shifted the mood? Her saying she didn't want dependency?

Surely he didn't want a clinging vine.

She didn't understand. All she knew was that he'd suddenly taken a step back, emotionally as well as physically. She watched in silence as he dropped back into his chair and released the brake.

Emotion over. Time to move back into medical mode.

And she needed to get back to Lily. Of course she did. There was no other choice.

'I'll see you soon,' she whispered.

'I guess you will,' he said, and his voice was even more formal. 'Keep Lily safe for me.' He took a deep breath. 'OK, now let's watch as all hell breaks loose.'

He'd been good to her, and it felt wrong.

He was in control, she thought as she made her way back through the hospital to Lily's ward. He'd stroked her hair, he'd raked her curls with his fingers, he'd set her back away from him, deciding they both needed to move on, he'd made her feel…protected.

She didn't want to feel protected, she thought suddenly, savagely. She wanted to feel…

Hot.

It was such an unexpected emotion that it had her stopping dead in the corridor and Beth, coming swiftly along the corridor behind her, almost bumped into the back of her.

'Whoops, sorry,' Beth said, and then she paused as she saw Jill's face. 'What's wrong?' And then, more urgently, 'Lily?'

'No,' Jill said, fast, though she tugged open Lily's door just to make sure. But Lily was just as she'd left her, sound asleep. The high colour in her cheeks had faded. Even from here she looked more normal. 'I think…'

'We all think,' Beth said solidly. 'We're all sure she'll be OK.'

'Robbie's not.'

'No,' Beth agreed gravely. 'He's not. Is that why you were looking like you were about to cry?'

'I wasn't.'

'Or is it Charles?' she said, more gently still.

'I… No.'

'I guess it's Charles,' Beth said softly, and then as Jill couldn't think of a reply, Beth caught her hand and lifted her ring to the light. 'It's a lovely ring,' she murmured, still watching Jill's face.

'It…it is.'

'You don't sound so sure.'

'It's just…' But she couldn't say. In truth, she didn't know. What was wrong with her? This was all just too complicated.

On the surface it had seemed easy. But when it got deeper it got hard. Too hard. And Beth was watching her, her eyes compassionate, waiting for a response.

'I think I want a husband,' Jill said at last, as if compelled to answer an unasked question. 'Not a medical superintendent.'

'Really?' Beth grinned. 'I can see you two playing doctors and nurses.' But her smile faded as she caught the fear in Jill's eyes. 'So what's wrong with that? I thought when I saw you yesterday morning…'

'I seduced him,' Jill said, and suddenly her voice was almost a wail. 'Of all the stupid, immature…'

'Wow!' Beth's eyes widened. Marcia came up behind them with an armload of linen. Beth grabbed Jill's arm and tugged her sideways into the tiny theatrette. 'Medical team meeting,' she said to a bemused Marcia. 'See that we're not disturbed.' She closed the door behind them.

'So you seduced him,' she said, leaning on the door in case Marcia couldn't resist joining in. 'And he submitted, kicking and screaming all the way.'

'Of course not. I shouldn't be saying…'

'No, that's just it,' Beth said. She left the door, put her hands on her friend's shoulders and pushed her back to sit on the examination couch. 'You never say. Neither of you. Look, I'm a newcomer here. A month working in Crocodile Creek and two weeks on this island is hardly enough for me to figure everything that's going on. But you two…everyone holds you in respect. You hold each other in respect. Here's Charles being so damned paternalistic…'

'He is, isn't he?'

'While you'd like him to take you to his lair, ravish you with red-hot kisses, smoulder you with molten desire…'

Jill blinked. 'Pardon?'

'Romance novels,' Beth said. 'I love 'em.'

'I don't think…'

'Come on, Jill, admit you wouldn't mind a bit of molten passion.'

'I did admit it,' she wailed. 'But now I feel stupid.'

'Because he's gone back to being paternalistic?'

'Yes!'

'Any particular reason?'

'I… Maybe I've brought it on myself,' she admitted. 'I mean…he knows I hate violence.' She shook her head. 'He's so kind. He was really kind to me just then. But I don't know…' She pushed her hair back from her face, trying to make her confused mind think.

She'd lost her hairband some time in the night and she hadn't had time to find a new one.

Lily was still asleep. She had time to fix her hair now. Get herself together. Stop being needy.

'He's a proud man,' Beth said thoughtfully.

'Yeah, and I'm a stupid woman,' Jill said. 'Beth, sorry. You were in the wrong place at the wrong time. Can we forget we had this conversation?'

'Sure,' Beth said, and her face softened. 'No. I'm not sure. I think you should keep talking. To Charles, if not to me. Tell him what you'd like.'

'See, that's just it,' Jill said, pushing herself to her feet. 'I don't know what it is that I would like.'

On the other side of the building Charles was having almost exactly the same conversation with Garf. Garf was confined to quarters and was bored enough to lie still and listen while Charles alternately barked orders into the phone and bellyached to the dog.

On the surface he was organising the logistics of the bio-hazard lab. A Black Hawk helicopter was on its way, loaded with gear designed to turn this place into an efficient, effective quarantine station. He had to be ready.

So he worked. In the gaps between phone calls he told Garf about Jill.

'I don't want her being kind,' he told the dog, and Garf made a strenuous effort to look intelligent.

'It's not that I don't want her, though.' He needed to say that, even though it was only to Garf. He wouldn't want even a dog to be getting the wrong idea.

For he definitely wanted her, he thought over and over as the arrangements for quarantine fell into place. Hell, he wanted her.

But on any terms?

She'd made love to him. Out of kindness?

Did he want that sort of loving?

Yes, a part of him shouted. He'd get what she was offering under any terms she cared to name.

But he knew it wasn't true. Even Garf was looking at him as if he knew it wasn't true. Gratitude... The last thing he wanted to think of when he was making love was how much he owed her.

It left a sour taste in his mouth which grew and grew.

How long could he stay married when the woman he loved felt sorry for him?

'And don't you feel sorry for me,' he told the soulful-eyed dog at his feet. 'Feel sorry for yourself. You're stuck within the campgrounds unless you're under supervision, to keep you away from the birds. Me...I'm just stuck.'

They were waiting for him outside, trying to decide on the site for the temporary lab. He had to go. He shoved his chair forward so hard that he misjudged the distance and hit the doorjamb. The metal from his chair's footrest took a neat wedge out of the skirting board.

'Good,' he said in grim satisfaction, and Garf eyed him with care, edged forward to his visitor's chair and gave the leg a tentative chew.

'Don't even think about it,' Charles warned him. 'I can be

destructive. Not you. Jill hates violence but me...I'm feeling more and more like violence. If I were you, dog, I'd be very good indeed.'

He shoved the door open. Garf gave a joyous leap toward freedom, only to be caught up by the length of rope round his neck.

'See,' Charles said grimly. 'Me and you both. Get used to it.'

Lily was definitely on the mend. By late that night she was sitting up in bed, sucking on flavoured ice, snuggling into Jill's arms and able to summon a smile when Charles wheeled through to see how she did.

'I've been really sick,' she whispered.

'You have,' Charles said, and his gut wrenched at the sight of how gaunt she'd become, and so fast. There was little enough of her at the best of times, but forty-eight hours of fever and no food had made her almost skeletal. 'Would you like something to eat?'

'No,' Lily said. And then, cautiously, she went on, 'Jelly beans?'

'Your wish is my command,' Charles said, thankful her request was something they always had at hand. He wheeled out to the nurses' station and came back with a handful.

'Not black ones.'

'I'll eat the black ones,' Jill said.

'They make your tongue go black.'

'So I'll have a scary tongue.'

He wanted them. Jill was sitting on the bed, smiling down at her little daughter, and he wanted them both so badly it was a physical pain. But Lily still had her IV line up. It wasn't safe to let her go back to the cabin yet, and Jill wouldn't go back to the cabin without Lily.

Maybe he could discharge her. For his own dishonourable reasons?

Of course he couldn't. Beth was Lily's doctor. He and Jill

needed to let Beth be in charge, do what she said, be parents instead of doctors.

'I want to go home,' Lily whispered.

'Not until Dr Beth says so,' Jill decreed, echoing his thoughts.

'Can Garf come and visit?'

'Not yet.'

'But he always visits the sick kids in camp.'

'You've got an illness that people might be able to catch,' Charles said. 'People can wash their hands and be careful about catching things. Garf would probably lick your face.'

Lily giggled. It was a tiny giggle but it sounded great. She snuggled against Jill, even closer than she had been. Possessive.

He put his hand out to stroke her cheek.

And then he flinched as light flooded the room. He turned to the window, just in time to see a blur of white—a man?—backing fast back into the darkness.

A photographer? What the hell…?

Media, he thought bitterly. They'd get photographs every way they could. This was huge. The possibility of bird flu would be on the front of every newspaper in the country.

'What was that?' Jill asked.

'I'll find out,' he said grimly, knowing his chances of stopping such intrusions were tiny. They needed security guards. They needed… Hell, they needed more resources than he could envisage. Quarantining a whole island…

'Will you sleep with me again tonight?' Lily asked Jill, and Charles knew her answer before she'd formed it.

'Of course.'

'That means you have to sleep all by yourself,' Lily said to Charles, and she sounded worried. 'Will you be scared?'

'No.'

'Will Garf sleep with you?'

'Of course he will,' Jill said soundly. 'Garf's the best dog in the world for stopping Charles being scared.' Her gaze met Charles's and held.

'He's Daddy,' Lily whispered, her eyelids drooping and the hand holding her jelly beans drooping as well, forcing Charles to wheel forward and take them from her. 'He's not Charles. He's Daddy.'

'That's right,' Jill said. 'Not Charles. Daddy.'

Was it a start? Maybe, but he sure as hell didn't want to be Daddy to Jill.

He lay in the too big bed that night and tried to concentrate on all the things that had to be done the next day. He was surrounded by chaos—furious guests from the resort, panicked camp parents, bureaucrats wanting answers, the media… There was so much for his mind to sort that the last thing it should be doing was sorting trivia.

Daddy.

It wasn't trivia, he thought. It was a fantastic start by Lily.

One down and one to go? He wanted to be Daddy to Lily. He wanted to be Charles to Jill. Not boss Charles or protector Charles or even friend Charles. He knew what he wanted.

He wanted the world.

CHAPTER ELEVEN

Monday was a blur. A crazy mix of high drama, bureaucracy, paperwork and personal involvement.

Even normal flu could be fatal in this set-up, Charles thought bleakly as he worked his way through everything the day threw at him. Like five-year-old Danny… Struggling to recover from cancer, infection led to almost lethal build-up in cranial pressure. Danny proved to be the exception to the quarantine rule—he had to be evacuated if he was to live. The protocols for getting that done proved a major headache.

Susie, their physiotherapist, was hit hard, the virus turning into potentially lethal pneumonia almost instantly. That shook the entire medical staff. Charles's job was to hold the team together, but watching Susie fight for her life shook even his steely control. Luckily the crisis was as short-lived as it was intense, but who knew who'd get ill next?

At least his own personal drama was lightening. Lily woke feeling better. As Charles wheeled in on his regular rounds she snuggled tight against her adoptive mother and peered at him with caution. And hope.

'Dr Beth says I can go home,' she whispered.

'To Croc Creek?'

'No, silly, to our bungalow,' Lily whispered, and snuggled against Jill some more. Jill kissed her hair and held her close, and Charles saw the glimmer of tears behind her tired eyes.

This self-contained woman was cracking inside. Opening to love?

Maybe, he thought. Maybe, he hoped. How far could she go?

'Maybe Charles can take us all home,' she whispered.

Lily considered. 'With Garf?'

'Maybe with Garf,' Charles said, and thought this felt great. Negotiating deals with his little daughter when two days ago he'd held grave fears for her life.

If only they could get past the acute stage with everyone. He'd heard from the hospital down south that Danny was starting to improve, but there were still two critically ill patients in the clinic and there were three more kids showing symptoms.

Dammit, there had to be a cause. Was it the birds?

'At least the biohazard lab's here now,' he told Jill. She'd been watching his face and he knew she was worrying about the same thing he was. 'Angus is starting tests on blood samples already. He's saying we might even have a result tonight.'

'As soon as that?'

'It'd be great,' he said. 'As long as…'

'As long as it's not bird flu?'

'There's a possibility it might be some sort of encephalitis,' he said. 'That's what Angus is thinking.'

'Isn't that caused by mosquitoes?'

'I've got a mosquito bite on my arm,' Lily said, and poked a skinny arm out to be inspected. 'It's itchy.'

They both grinned at one red bump on one skinny arm— a medical imperative where the imperative had been much, much more frightening. And suddenly they were grinning at each other.

Only Jill backed off. Her smile started wide and free, but suddenly it was like she remembered she had no right to feel like that.

What would it take to have her relax with him again? It was like she'd taken one huge step over her boundary, scared herself stupid and retreated.

Well, if she thought he was staying on his side of the wall…

He had to, he thought grimly. Rushing her… There was no way he could.

'Dr Wetherby?' It was Marcia, calling from the corridor. 'Robbie's mother's on the phone from Melbourne. Can you speak to her?'

He winced. Robbie's mum had four other children, all younger than Robbie. She was desperately frightened to have Robbie ill and so far away.

'I'll ring her back in five minutes,' he told Marcia. 'Meanwhile ask her if she can get on to the Internet. Beth's with him—right? She's being almost a surrogate mother to him. I'll grab the digital camera. A picture of Beth cuddling him might do his mum more good than any reassurance I can give.'

'It should,' Marcia said, smiling her agreement. 'We have so many doctors we can almost have one-on-one attention. Robbie has Dr Beth. Susie has Dr Vavunis. Our Lily here has you two.'

'They're my mum and dad,' Lily said firmly.

Charles smiled. But then he glanced at Jill and his smile faded.

She looked fearful.

She wouldn't believe in happiness, he thought. Would she spend the rest of her life not believing she could move out of the shadows?

Even though they had an over-supply of doctors, there was still a mass of work that only he could do. But he did manage to go with Jill and Lily late that afternoon when Beth decreed Lily could return to the bungalow. She'd lost her bounce, he thought as he watched Jill carry her up the steps. In all the time they'd cared for her, Lily had refused to be carried. Even when she'd fallen off her swing and given herself a greenstick fracture of the arm four months ago, she'd refused to be held.

Now she was clinging so tightly to Jill that he was worried

all over again. And when he said he had to return to the clinic her face crumpled into tears.

'I want you to stay.'

'Charles has to go,' Jill said, trying to sound firm.

'I'll be back tonight,' he said.

'When tonight?' Lily demanded fiercely. 'To read me a bedtime story?'

'I'll try.'

'It's not fair,' she whined.

'We're fine alone,' Jill said, and they all had to regroup after that.

This family business was getting complicated.

Be careful what you wish for, Charles thought ruefully as he wheeled back along the path leading to the beach. The bio-hazard lab was just up from the cove. He'd just check with Angus to see how things were going.

Things weren't going. 'It'll be some hours,' Angus told him. 'I'll let you know. Will you be in your bungalow?'

'I might be. Or I might be sitting outside this damned lab, just waiting.'

And in the end that's where he was. For medical imperatives took over and by the time he returned to the bungalow both Lily and Jill were asleep.

Together in the big bed.

We're fine alone.

They didn't stir as he wheeled silently into the bedroom. Stealth on wheels—that's how his junior staff described him. He wheeled in and looked across the bed at his future wife and his daughter, their heads just touching on the one pillow.

What would a normal father do? Wake them up? Ask them to shove aside, climb in beside them, cuddle them both and fall asleep? It was so far out of his orbit that it seemed unimaginable.

There was an empty room in the clinic now Danny had

been evacuated. He'd sleep in there. If anyone asked he'd tell them he wanted to be around when the results came through.

He did want to be around when the results came through.

He gazed for another long moment at the woman and child peacefully sleeping and his mouth twisted. So near…

It was an impossible ask. The familiarity of family. Where the hell did one start?

Not here. Not now.

'Goodnight,' he whispered, but they didn't stir.

He turned and went out into the night. To sit outside a lab and wait.

It was better than waiting for what might never happen.

And as he went Jill's eyes opened. She stared bleakly out through the darkened doorway.

What sort of stupid cowardice had kept her silent?

What sort of cowardice was driving her forward?

The results came through at ten. The door of the lab opened. Angus came out, leading Beth by the hand. Joyous.

Charles was sitting back a little so he could look out over the moonlit sea as he waited. Their body language spoke of triumph. And more.

Here was another one, he thought bleakly. Another Croc Creek romance.

But at least the news they carried was good. Great!

They approached him with concern. 'Are you all right?' was the first question Beth asked as they approached him, and he thought he must seem a figure for sympathy. Sitting alone late at night, waiting for test results. He normally slept little but he'd slept so little in the last few days that he knew his face must be showing signs of strain. And Beth was a doctor who saw beyond the surface.

'Should I be?' he said wearily. 'We've had an outbreak of a potentially fatal disease on the island. I've my ward—my daughter—Lily in hospital, we've had to break quarantine to fly a desperately ill child to the mainland...'

She didn't believe his reasons. He watched her face and he knew she was thinking of Jill. That was his penance for employing good doctors, he thought. He should try employing a few who treated outward symptoms and didn't go fishing where they weren't wanted.

'At least we can take one load off your shoulders,' Angus said gently. 'It's not bird flu. I can show you the screens if you like—I've left them up. The genetic make-up of whatever we have here is totally different to bird flu. In fact, it's not flu at all. We're back to mosquitoes and encephalitis, and even though that has severe consequences it's not the start of some pandemic. We can raise the quarantine—people can leave the island.'

Encephalitis. A blood-borne virus carried by mosquitoes.

'It makes sense,' Charles said slowly, thinking it through. 'Even though we had to take precautions over bird flu, we've been thinking further. We had a vast number of trees uprooted in the cyclone. Where they came out we've got depressions in the ground that have filled with water and made ideal mosquito breeding grounds. Also, with the fierce winds of the cyclone... If it's encephalitis I'm guessing there's been some different strain of mosquito blown down from the northern islands.' He shook his head. 'Too easy. We can get the depressions filled. It's such a contained area we can do a spray. The dry season will get rid of the last of them... We just have to weather this patch.'

'And we'll all live happily ever after,' Angus said.

'Yeah,' he agreed and tried to look cheerful. 'Thank you both,' he said. 'Doing the lab work was dangerous.'

'It had its compensations,' Angus said, and Charles glanced at Beth, who blushed and grinned.

'Right,' he said dryly.

'Will you tell Jill now?' Beth asked, and once again he had the feeling that Beth saw too much. His staff accused him of having second sight. Here he was on the other side of the fence, and he wasn't enjoying it one bit.

'I guess. If she's awake,' he said brusquely. 'But there's a thousand phone calls to make before then. I need to get on.'

And he wheeled away, leaving them to their happiness.

He spent an hour on the phone contacting all relevant authorities. He also contacted Mike Poulos, the helicopter pilot, who was here with his wife Emily. Mike had been going quietly nuts, worrying that Emily could catch whatever this was. In the first trimester of pregnancy, treating her would be really problematic.

Even though the need no longer seemed urgent, Charles knew the only way Mike would relax would be if he could get her off the island. He made the call and twenty minutes later watched the helicopter take off.

Emily was still protesting. 'This is crazy. I can wear insect repellent. It's the middle of the night. I'm not an emergency.'

But Mike's face said it all. He loved Emily so fiercely that a middle-of-the-night flight meant nothing.

Here it was again. Gut-wrenching envy as Charles watched them go.

The media was next but he was so tired he couldn't think straight. He could go to sleep in Mike and Emily's bungalow, he thought, but maybe, just maybe, Jill was worrying.

So he went. The cabin was in darkness. He wheeled through into the bedroom and Jill and Lily were curled up together in the big bed.

Were they asleep? He hesitated but Jill's eyes opened. She gazed across at him in the moonlight. Soundlessly she slipped out of bed and padded over the bare floorboards.

She was gorgeous, he thought, and the ache that had been in his gut for the past few days grew even fiercer. In her T-shirt and knickers, her curls tangled around her shoulders, her feet bare… She was the woman of his dreams. She'd given him a taste of paradise but had then withdrawn. How to get her back? Was it fair to even try?

They mustn't disturb Lily. He turned the chair and wheeled outside. She followed him out onto the veranda.

'Lily wanted to sleep with me,' she whispered, sounding defensive.

'Of course.'

'I'll…I'll move her onto the settee now.'

'But she might wake up,' he said, and waited for her to disagree.

She didn't.

'It's OK,' he said gently. 'There's a cabin spare. Mike flew Emily out tonight—you know she's in the early stages of pregnancy? We've confirmed it's not bird flu.'

'Oh, Charles,' she whispered. 'That's wonderful.'

'It's not bad,' he said, and managed a smile. 'But Mike still wanted to get her off the island as fast as possible. It may not be bird flu but it's still a nasty bug.'

'What do you think it is?'

'Angus is saying some sort of encephalitis caused by mosquitoes. We won't wait for confirmation—we'll have an eradication team start tomorrow.'

'You'll take Zach and Dom off dead-bird duty?'

He gave a wry smile. 'If I didn't think their father would get the hell out of here the minute he gets the news that quarantine's been lifted, I'd have them culling mosquitoes by hand.'

'Thank you,' she said simply.

'I think I've told you before,' he said, almost roughly. 'I don't want your thanks.'

'What do you want?'

'You,' he said, so savagely that he startled them both.

'You can't want me,' she whispered, sounding awed.

'What the hell do you mean by that?'

'I'm not…' She bit her lip. 'Just because you're in a wheelchair…'

It was the wrong thing to say. The words hung in the stillness, a tangible, awful truth. There was a moment's appalled silence.

'It always comes down to that,' Charles said, and even though he'd lowered his voice the savagery was even more intense. 'It always comes down to the bloody wheelchair.'

'I didn't mean that.' She could barely get the words out. Her face was blanched of all colour and she shrank back against the balustrade.

'You said it.'

His phone buzzed. It had been buzzing non-stop all night. He shouldn't be here, he thought savagely. There were a million things he should be doing.

He glanced at Jill's distressed face and thought even more definitely that he shouldn't be there.

It was the head of one of the nation's largest media outlets.

'My journalists are having trouble getting through to you,' the man snapped. 'I need an in-depth interview before we roll the presses, Charles. There's rumours flying everywhere that you've got something worse than bird flu.'

'I'll be in my office in ten minutes,' he said wearily. 'I'll do a teleconference if you want to set it up. Not just you, though, David. The opposition as well.'

'I want an exclusive.'

'Don't we all,' Charles snapped, more harshly than he'd intended. Looking at Jill.

He replaced his phone in his pocket. Jill was looking distressed and confused and…frightened? It took only that, he thought bleakly. She was frightened of him?

'How's Robbie?' she whispered. 'And Susie?'

OK. If she wanted to move back to medicine—safe ground—then maybe he had no choice but to follow.

'No one's worse,' he told her. 'We're thinking they'll be OK. We're figuring this bug out now. Fluids, fever control and antivirals on first symptoms. Those who showed the first signs yesterday aren't getting sicker. Mosquito repellent will be compulsory as of first thing tomorrow and hopefully the scare will be over. I have to go.'

'Of course you do,' she whispered. 'Charles…what I said…about the wheelchair…'

'Forget it,' he said roughly. 'I just wish to hell I could.'

She hadn't meant it. She sat on the balustrade and stared out into the night, replaying the conversation over and over in her head.

He'd said he wanted her. And she'd said, *Just because you're in a wheelchair…*

He'd taken it to be some sort of rejection. And in a way it was, she thought bleakly. Just because he was in a wheelchair he was restricted to the likes of her.

Only…he hadn't been thinking that. She knew that. Her words had been meant to be an apology. Instead he'd taken them as a slap.

She should go after him. Set it right.

She couldn't, of course. Lily was here. Lily was asleep in her bed.

She could have lifted Lily onto the settee and taken Charles into her bed. Exposed her neediness again…

It was just as well he was needed elsewhere, she thought as she returned to her too big bed to face the demons of the night. She wanted… She wanted..

What did she want?

She wanted him to be well, she thought fiercely. She wanted him to be whole and wonderful and able to choose a mate worthy of him.

Because she loved him.

She hugged her arms across her breasts and shivered, even though the night was warm and still.

How could she figure this out? How could she possibly make herself someone he deserved?

* * *

'Someone's left a flower for Lily.'

It was Marcia, cheerfully pushing the screen door wide to find Jill and Lily having breakfast. Lily was propped up on pillows and Jill was feeding her toast fingers dipped in egg. For a fiercely independent little girl, this was an admission of need indeed, and Marcia's eyes widened.

'Wow! I wish someone would feed me toast fingers. And leave me flowers.' She set the flower on the bedside table and grinned down at Lily. 'I think you might have a boyfriend.'

'I have lots of boyfriends,' Lily said serenely. 'Which one?'

'I saw Sam running back toward the camp,' Marcia told her, grinning at Jill.

'I like Sam,' Lily said. So did they all. The little boy was in his second remission from acute lymphoblastic leukaemia, but no amount of medical battering could conquer his indomitable spirit. 'He isn't sick?'

'No more sickies this morning,' Marcia reported. 'But Charles has called a meeting of all staff. Jill, he'd like you there. Lily, is it OK if I sit with you while Jill spends a little time in the hospital?'

'She's not Jill,' Lily said, and dropped her spoon and lunged forward to grab Jill round the waist. 'She's my mum.'

Jill blinked. She now had egg all over her T-shirt. She had a clingy little girl to contend with and Lily had never clung.

She was a mum.

'Hey,' Marcia said, and smiled, a trifle mistily. All the Crocodile Creek staff knew Lily's story. More people than Jill and Charles had worried about her fierce independence. This was a new Lily.

Maybe it wouldn't last past convalescence, but maybe…just maybe there'd been a breakthrough.

'I'll be gone for an hour at most, poppet,' Jill murmured, and Lily pulled back and glared.

'Promise?'

'I promise.' She glanced apologetically at Marcia. 'If I can be spared.'

'You're officially on leave, starting now,' Marcia said. 'We've decided. You were never meant to be here anyway. You need to stop being Director of Nursing for a bit while you learn to be a mum. But after Charles's meeting,' she said apologetically. 'Now, I think you need to change your T-shirt and I need to make your daughter another egg.'

They were in contact with the outside world. Jill walked into the meeting room and was assailed by news.

The big screen television was on, and Wallaby Island was the news of the day. There were pictures of Beth on the screen, with Angus. And Garf, being ridiculous. 'Medical authorities in charge of the suspected bird flu epidemic,' the voice-over was saying, and Jill looked at Beth's image in gorgeous blue pyjamas and smiled in sympathy. The media took whatever angle they wanted.

But then the image changed. 'Dr Charles Wetherby, Medical Director, with his fiancée and child,' the voice-over was saying, and there they were, framed as a family by Lily's bedside. Charles was touching her cheek. Jill's cheek. She remembered him touching her. Her hand flew involuntarily to her cheek now, remembering.

He looked like he loved her.

She swallowed hard while those around her turned and smiled in sympathy.

She glanced away, down at the table. Newspapers… Mike, she thought. He must have returned this morning after taking Emily off the island and had brought back the world's news.

And on the front cover…

This was yesterday's newspaper, she thought, dazed. A photograph taken—by who? She didn't remember. She was cradling Lily in her arms. Lily looked ill almost to the death. Jill was holding her close, looking down into her face with despair

The photograph was huge, almost bigger than real life.

'The Human Cost of a Pandemic', the caption read.

Fear gripped her. Cold and hard and terrible. This was what she'd spent the last eight years trying to avoid.

Kelvin.

She'd changed her name. She'd spent the last eight years hiding. But there was no hiding this. She lifted the paper and underneath was another newspaper. A daily national broadsheet. A different caption.

Same photograph.

He had to see this.

He'd never let this go.

'Jill?' She dropped the newspaper and turned. Charles.

'What is it?' he said. And then more urgently, 'Jill?'

'I…'

'What?' He glanced down at the table and saw what she'd been seeing. 'The papers?'

'Kelvin,' she whispered.

'Hey.' He understood, she thought. One fast glance at the headlines brought comprehension. 'Jill, don't look like that,' he said. 'It's been eight years. He's in jail.'

'He isn't any more. At least, I don't think so.'

'You don't know. You're on a remote island.' And then, more urgently, 'You have me.'

'You don't know what he's like,' she said dully. 'I have to leave.'

'Of course you don't have to leave.'

'He'll hurt Lily. He'll destroy us.'

'Jill, this is paranoid.'

'It's not. I have to go. For Lily's sake.'

'It's OK,' he said, sternly. 'Let's not overreact. I'll talk to Harry.'

'He won't be able to stop him.'

'Jill, he can't be that bad.'

'He is.'

'Then we'll talk to Harry,' he said. 'Harry can move heaven and earth for the people he cares about, and he cares about you. We all do. He'll find out where he is and we'll go from there.'

The terror lessened. Just a fraction. If she could know where he was…

'He'll do that?'

'Let's ask him,' Charles said strongly, and took her hand. 'But you're not to look like that. Jill, I need to talk to the staff about what's happening, and the nursing questions about encephalitis would be better directed to you.'

'Of course. I shouldn't have worried you.'

'Of course you should have worried me,' he said strongly. 'If I'm to be your husband… Hell, I'm worried already.'

Harry took her seriously as well.

'We'll put a track on him straight away,' he said. 'With his criminal record, even if he's out he's likely to be subject of a parole order. Meanwhile you concentrate on getting your little girl well again. Leave Kelvin to Charles and to me.'

'But—'

'We won't let him hurt you,' Charles said, softly but with quiet assurance. 'I promise.'

She had to be content with that.

She listened while Charles outlined the precautions staff were to take to prevent any more cases of encephalitis. Bush walks were off the agenda until the waterholes were filled. Insect repellent was to be worn by everyone. But now they knew, the island could be made safe. The camp staff could go back to the job at hand. Which was making sick kids feel great.

'Which means this is a beach day,' Melissa, the activity director, decreed. 'There's no mossies near the beach. We'll set up shade sails, with a few camp beds for those who need a rest. We'll have beach games, a reef walk and a barbecue. Let's get these bad few days behind us.'

She didn't say what everyone here knew. For many of these kids life was precarious. You didn't wait around until everything was perfect before having fun. Perfect might never happen.

'Now we know the kids with the virus aren't contagious, they can be included if they're well enough,' Melissa went on. 'Some of the kids have been frightened. They've watched Danny and Lily and Robbie get sick. We need reassurance. Jill, what if we brought you and Lily down to the beach in a buggy for a couple of hours? Lily could lie on a camp bed and watch. She wouldn't have to join in. I could tell the kids she was resting and she could watch from a distance.'

'That'd be great,' Charles said warmly, smiling at Jill, and she knew he was thinking it'd be great for her as well. It'd get her out of the bungalow. Away from her fears.

'Fine,' she said weakly.

'We'll both be there,' Charles said. 'Life gets back to normal. Starting now.'

They'd had enough dramas. They should have been able to relax for the next few days.

It didn't happen.

Charles worked until after lunch and then came back to the bungalow just as Lily woke up. The little girl was pale and weary but when Jill suggested they take the beach buggy down to the sea, she reacted with pleasure.

'With both of you?'

'Yes.'

'With my mummy and my daddy,' she said, and smiled a secret smile.

Jill felt like crying. It was so good. It was almost perfect. Except for the fact that she and Charles were still absurdly formal.

And out there somewhere was Kelvin.

But she was able to forget that on the beach. Almost every kid in camp was there, and most of the staff as well. There were also guests from the resort. Normally the resort guests kept to their part of the island, but Benita Green, the cancer nurse had invited resort kids to share in the reef walk if they wanted.

They did want. For everyone on the island, it felt like a holiday, a release from the threat that had hung over them briefly but terribly. Even the few photographers snapping in the distance didn't feel like a threat.

For they stayed apart. Benita had set up a shade sail solely for their use, tucked discreetly to the side of the first of the sand-hills so the rest of the kids couldn't see Lily was there. Lily wasn't up to joining in just yet, and neither did she want to. Here they could lie side by side and watch everything on the beach without Lily tiring.

That was another blinking moment for Jill as she saw the set-up. Benita, Beth—everyone in camp knew the pressure they'd been under.

This was a gesture to their embryonic family.

'I'm in the middle,' Lily said importantly so they lay on the lounges on either side of their daughter, and Jill caught Charles's gaze over Lily's head and they shared a smile that took her breath away.

It felt so good. Just to lie here as a family… Maybe it could work, she thought as they soaked up the sun. Maybe it just needed time. Maybe—

A scream broke the stillness. She looked toward the sea, startled. Benita, the cancer care nurse, was in the shallows, surrounded by a gaggle of assorted kids. Sam had broken away from the group, running up the beach as if terrified, a skinny little kid in scant bathers, holding his towel like it contained something precious.

But his run faltered. As she watched, he screamed again. The towel fell at his feet and he stared at it in horror.

And crumpled where he stood.

Sam!

'You stay. I'll go,' Charles snapped. She'd hardly reacted before Charles was in the buggy.

'They might need—'

'The beach is covered with medics.' Charles was already shoving the buggy into gear. 'Take care of Lily while I see what's happening.'

Charles moved fast but in this crowd from the medical camp and the medical conference, it was inevitable that other medics got there before him.

Beth reached Sam first, falling onto her knees beside him, moving into reflex airway check.

'Get the kids back,' she snapped as Charles got within hearing range. 'Do you know what happened?'

'He just screamed and fell down,' Benita said, appalled.

Beth was holding Sam's wrist. His chest was barely moving. How could he go from a laughing, running child to this in seconds?

'I'll take his towel,' one of the kids said uncertainly, and Beth and Angus, and Charles, too, speeding along the beach to join them, had the same thought at exactly the same moment.

'Don't touch it.'

Respiratory arrest? It had to be.

At least there were enough doctors here, and then some. Sam was in the best of hands but Charles felt helpless. Beth was already breathing for the little boy, pinching his nose and breathing into his mouth, short, sharp bursts of air, her head turning as she breathed so she could watch his chest move as she filled it for him. It was expired air but it was the best they could offer until they could get oxygen. Angus was by her side, ready to assist.

What had caused this? Charles turned his cart toward Sam's towel. But once again he and Beth were thinking alike.

Angus had taken over Sam's breathing and the moment he did, Beth grabbed a piece of driftwood and poked at the towel. It fell open, and a shell rolled sideways onto the sand.

'That's a cone shell.' It was an onlooker—a stranger. There were too many people on the beach but at least this one seemed sensible. The stranger strode forward and stood protectively over the shell, as if to stop anyone else being inadvertently stung.

A cone shell… Dear God.

This was the geographer cone. Charles had read about them. He'd seen pictures but he'd never seen one in real life. Neither had he ever wanted to. A thing of exquisite beauty, the fish inside shot poison through a series of toothed harpoons in the narrow end of the shell. The venom could kill almost instantly. The fine harpoons could even be directed backwards toward the fat end of the shell, and a direct sting could kill a man.

What was it doing on this sheltered, netted beach? It was extremely rare in these waters. It must have been washed here in the storm. For Sam to find it…

It was a nightmare.

And there was nothing Charles could do. Angus was working as well as any doctor could, a big, competent doctor moving into emergency mode with practised precision, pinching Sam's tiny, snubbed nose and breathing into his mouth, over and over, short, sharp bursts of air.

Where was the medical cart? He lifted his phone and barked orders, telling Luke that fast wasn't fast enough. They had to have oxygen. Now!

Beth was examining Sam's hands, searching for what they knew had to be there.

'Here!' It was a tiny red welt on his little finger. There was no doubting it now. One of the barbs had dug right in.

Charles turned and glanced up the beach. Jill was holding Lily, and he could see Lily's distress as well. The body language of everyone on the beach told its own story.

Sam had to live. It was too far for him to see Jill's expression from here—or to listen to Lily's distress—but they both knew Sam.

Sam was almost family. Charles's embryonic family was too small as it was.

Sam had to live.

Jill had to take Lily home. There were too many people on the beach already. She couldn't see what was happening. She wasn't needed. Charles would do what needed to be done. Charles and his team. And if the worst happened…

Lily was sobbing in distress, having heard enough from the shouting, from the terrified yells of the kids, to know that Sam was in danger. She was frantic for Sam, desperate to know what was happening.

'I think something's stung him,' Jill told her, cradling her in her arms, wanting to know herself but fearing that taking Lily closer might be—would be—crazy. 'But the doctors are taking care of him. I think we should go home.'

'Will Sam die?'

'Charles is looking after him.'

'My daddy is looking after him,' Lily corrected her, sounding suddenly stern, and the fear in her voice faded a little. 'Daddy will make him better.'

Luke arrived faster than could reasonably be expected, barrelling down the track from the camp in the medical cart, bringing much-needed equipment. Oxygen. Analgesics. It must have been pain that had caused Sam to collapse so dramatically, Charles thought as he watched his team in action. Shock would have sent him into incipient cardiac arrest, thankfully now reversed.

Sometimes it was hard to be the boss, he thought bleakly. These young doctors were great. He'd hand-picked his team and he trusted them, but sometimes it'd be easier to get in there and do the work himself.

But Sam looked as if he was coming out the other side. There was no need for him to intervene.

As Angus slid a cannula into the back of Sam's hand and prepared to give him morphine, the little boy's eyes fluttered open.

Just momentarily but enough to give them all hope.

Now they had oxygen going and breathing established they could afford to take their time—in fact, it was better to try and stabilise him before they moved him. With the immediate medical imperatives covered there was now time to take in the whole scene. To one side lay Sam's towel, discarded. The stranger was still standing over it—seemingly protective. In its midst lay the cone shell, a cylindrical whirl of beauty. Tangerine and cream and black, perfectly patterned. Deadly.

How the hell…? He'd had divers go over every inch of the cove before he'd let the kids swim here. The nets had been broken in the storm, but he'd had the cove checked again afterwards.

He closed his eyes. Not securely enough, obviously.

'You want me to take care of it?'

The stranger was a thick-set guy in his forties or fifties. Unlike most of the people on the beach he was fully clothed and wearing thick boots and hat. Charles took in his appearance in some surprise. This guy looked as if he worked outdoors. His hat was battered and grubby. He didn't look like a tourist.

'I'm a fisherman here on holiday,' he said, answering Charles's question before he uttered it. 'I make my living fishing for abalone. I know how to cope with this.'

'My rangers will—'

'Do your guys know what range these things will sting from?' the man said. He walked across to the nearest shade sail, tugged it out of the ground and brought it over. 'They can stay alive for hours out of water, but a few layers of canvas'll do it,' he said. 'I'll wrap it up so tight nothing can get near it. Tell me where to take it.'

'We have a medical disposal unit at the back of the hospital,' Charles said, grateful for the man's practical assurances. 'I'll send a ranger down to help you.'

'I'll be right here.'

He nodded, grateful. Hell, he'd had enough drama. He was feeling sick. But Sam's colour was returning. They had the best medical staff on the island and he knew that it was sheer skill that had saved Sam's life.

Maybe they'd got past this threat, too.

Please.

Jill took Lily back to the cabin. They were silent on the way back, awed and frightened by what they'd seen.

'But he won't die,' Lily kept saying. 'He won't die.'

'Of course he won't die.'

'It's lucky we have Daddy.'

'It is.'

They paused when they reached the bungalow. There was a small brown dog sitting on the doorstep. A stuffed toy. Ritz. This cute little dog with his top hat and cane played his crazy song and did a little dance every time someone pressed his foot. He was the camp mascot.

'Someone's trying to make you feel better,' she told Lily, and Lily picked up the little dog and smiled and pressed his foot.

'But I don't need him,' she said softly as Ritz danced. 'Lots of kids at camp don't have mummies and daddies here. They need Ritz more than I do.'

'That's lovely,' Jill whispered, feeling choked. She set the little dog on the bench by the door. Even though he was gorgeous, he wasn't a toy to take to bed and cuddle. The heavy musical mechanism in his base made him more of a paperweight. 'I'll take him back later.'

She'd show Charles first, though, she thought. She'd tell him what Lily had said.

Lots of kids here don't have mummies and daddies.

Lily had moved on.

Maybe…maybe…

She wanted him to come. Maybe all her fears were irrational.

Lily was asleep almost as soon as her head hit the pillow. It was a skill of childhood—moving from being awake to the deepest of sleep in an instant. Jill was almost jealous.

She couldn't sleep. She was left alone with her thoughts.

How soon till Charles came?

The screen door swung open behind her in the living room, and she smiled. She left the sleeping Lily and walked out to meet him. 'Charles, you'll never guess what Lily said—'

It wasn't Charles.

It was Kelvin.

'Sam's going to be OK?' Harry, like everyone at the resort, was appalled by what had happened. The big policeman met Charles as he walked out of the treatment room, his tanned face drawn and worried.

'He's looking good,' Charles told him. 'He must have only got a tiny sting through the towel. The barbs didn't stick. But when I think of what could have happened… It's my job to keep this place safe. How the hell—?'

'It's what happens,' Harry said, gripping his friend's shoulder in concern. 'You know that. It's life. You can keep these kids in cotton wool for the rest of their lives or you can give them a camp like this one. With risks.'

'I had no right—'

'The risks were tiny,' Harry said. 'The encephalitis was dead unlucky and so was the cone shell. I just did a search on the Internet, finding out about them. They're rare as hens' teeth on this coast. It must have been blasted down during the cyclone. There's been one recorded death in all of Australia history. Sam had better odds of being abducted by aliens than of being stung by one of these.'

'Don't say it,' Charles begged. 'The way I'm feeling, you're tempting fate. Any minute aliens will land.'

'If they do, we'll pick them up on the way in,' Harry assured him. 'I've got the base covered. Any arrivals get vetted before they set foot on the island.'

'Kelvin?'

'Jill's not a woman to scare easily. From what I'm hearing, she's right to be scared.'

'Hell.' He was starting to feel overwhelmed.

'We'll keep her safe,' Harry said. 'I've had his photograph faxed through and I've just taken copies down to the jetty. The ferry staff will notify me the minute they see him—well before he gets near the island. We'll saturate the district with his image. I left one in your office. Can you show Jill and tell her what we're doing?' He gripped Charles's shoulder once more. 'It's OK. The run of bad luck ends here.'

He left him, striding out of the hospital looking purposeful and competent. He was a good man to have on side, Charles thought. Jill could relax with Harry taking care of her.

Harry rather than him? Yeah, he thought grimly. He was feeling sick with frustration. No matter what Harry said, he'd failed to protect the people who were depending on him.

He had to phone Sam's parents.

Who'd want to be a medical director? Not him. Not now. He felt weary to the bone.

He wheeled forward into his office and lifted the receiver. While he dialled he glanced idly at the photograph Harry had left on the desk.

He dropped the phone.

CHAPTER TWELVE

IT WAS the nightmare she'd known must finally happen. If she ever left he'd kill her. He'd said it so often she heard it in her dreams.

It had hung over her, even as she'd built her career, as she'd fallen in love with Lily. As she'd fallen in love with Charles.

'I told you I'd come,' he said, almost pleasantly, and she saw what he was carrying and she almost fainted.

He was wearing gloves. Thick leather gloves that covered his arms to the wrist. She remembered he'd worn them when the winches had got stuck, when he'd had to haul fishing lines in by hand.

He must have his boat here, she thought, feeling sick. Somehow he had his fishing gear. So he had his protective gloves.

He was holding Sam's cone shell with all the reverence in the world.

'Just lucky, eh?' he said. 'I saw your picture in the paper and I had the boat in Cairns. It was dead easy to bring the boat into one of the coves along the coast. So I was watching you playing happy families on the beach. With the cripple. I sat there on the beach away from the crowd, trying to figure it out. I've done enough years behind bars on your account. There's no one going to point the finger at me for your murder—or even if they do, they won't be able to prove it.'

'What…what do you mean?'

'Natural causes,' he said sardonically, and he tossed the shell a couple of inches in the air and caught it with casual care. 'Yeah, people will have seen me on the beach. I know that. So I took the shell and came inland to dispose of it like a good little citizen. On the way I met my ex-wife—after all, you were the reason I was here. I wanted to apologise for all that past rubbish. Anyway, you wanted to have a look and I was so dumb I showed it to you and you just touched it—'

'No!'

'Nothing to it,' he said mildly. 'I wonder if the kid touched it, too?'

'No!'

'Ugly cow,' he said. He was walking steadily toward her, forcing her to back into the bedroom. Blessedly Lily was deeply asleep, exhausted with the combination of illness and shock from the scene on the beach. Please, God, she wouldn't wake up.

'Kelvin, don't do this,' Jill whispered, trying to keep her voice steady. 'There's nothing to gain and everything to lose.'

'I won't lose anything,' he said. 'I spent five years in the slammer over you. Five years! You think you should get off scot-free?'

'I didn't.'

'No,' he said, staring at her, taking in how she looked now. 'Look at you. Ugly as sin. Even uglier than you were when your old man forced me to marry you. Women get old faster than men and you're getting old faster than most. It's a wonder you can get any man to look at you, even the miserable cripple you've finally latched on to.' And he moved toward her with the shell.

'Jill could have any man she looked at,' Charles said strongly from the living room, and Jill's gaze flew past Kelvin. Shock piling on shock. Charles had come in silently. He was in his wheelchair, just inside the living-room door, maybe fifteen feet from Kelvin.

He was simply sitting, watching the events in the bedroom with his usual calmness.

'H-he's g-got the shell,' Jill stuttered, and Charles nodded.

'I can see he's got the shell. What I want to know is, how on earth can he aim it at you if he's blind?'

'What the hell do you mean by that?' Kelvin snarled.

Charles didn't pose a threat, Jill thought. Kelvin had moved sideways a little so he could see them both, but his face showed no alarm. In fact, there was almost a hint of satisfaction.

He'd kill Charles, too, Jill thought in panic. He could. He was a big man, at the height of his physical powers. He was armed with something as lethal as a gun.

'I mean Jill's the sexiest, most desirable, most wonderful woman I've ever had the privilege to meet,' Charles said, as if this was a normal conversation, with a normal man, and he was telling the world of the woman he was to marry. He lifted Ritz, the crazy little dog, from the bench by the door and looked down at him with affection. 'She's given me a family. Jill, Lily, friends, dogs, toys… I have a family now, with Jill at its heart.'

The pride in his voice was unmistakable and Jill's eyes widened in shock.

'Don't…' she whispered.

'Don't tell Kelvin what a fool he was for having you and losing you? For not knowing what a gift he had, if only he'd treated you as you deserved to be treated? He has a whole body. He was capable of giving you the loving you deserved and he squandered it.'

'Oh, Charles,' she whispered. 'As if you're not capable—'

'Shut the hell up,' Kelvin yelled, clearly rattled by a conversation he didn't understand. And then he laughed. 'Sorry. I should be more generous. Any last words, or something like that?'

'Don't be a fool,' Charles said. 'I've called the police. They know what you intend. Your only chance is to lay the shell down and walk away. Fast.'

'Right,' Kelvin jeered, and took two fast steps toward Jill and grabbed her by the hair. He tugged her hard against him and raised the shell in his free hand. 'Her first and then you. She's touched the shell and it speared her; you came in and were so upset you just grabbed her, like they did with the kid on the beach. I tried to warn you the shell was under her—'

'Leave her,' Charles said sharply.

'Watch me,' he said, and he raised the shell slightly higher, its lethal end poised and ready to fall…

But then…

It came from nowhere, a brown blur of fur and metal, Ritz, hurled across the room with all the force of Charles's strong arm. Years of pushing his wheelchair, of holding himself up on his elbow crutches, of depending on his arms for everything, had given him strength that was almost uncanny.

And deadly accuracy.

The shell was exposed, in the palm of Kelvin's hand, held high, and Charles didn't miss. The shell smashed where it was held, with a cracking thud, spattering shell and fish fragments everywhere.

And Charles was there. His wheelchair followed through with savage ferocity, smashing into Kelvin's legs, hurling him backward beside the bed.

His hand was still grasping Jill's hair, hauling her down. Charles grabbed her arm and wrenched her away with such force he must have come close to dislocating her shoulder, and Kelvin had no chance to hold her.

'Get back,' he yelled at her, but there was no need, for the force of his pull had her stumbling behind him, sprawling to the floor.

And Kelvin didn't follow. Instead he screamed. His gloved hand clutched his face—and he screamed again.

'Don't touch anything,' Charles barked at him. 'Stay still.'

But Kelvin was clutching his face as if it burned, crumpling to his knees. The broken shell must have spattered against his face, piercing the skin. The geographer cone was one of the most deadly of sea creatures and if it smashed, even a tiny scratch would let venom in. Kelvin's hands had been protected by the gloves. Involuntarily he was clutching his face with his hands, pushing smashed shell against his skin, spreading more of the venom.

Jill staggered upright, appalled. 'I'll get—'

'Get in the shower,' Charles snapped at her, hauling back from the man on the floor, shoving his chair between Jill and Kelvin. 'Now. Use a towel to open the shower door and to turn on the tap. You'll have stuff on you. You don't know if you've got scratches anywhere. Don't touch your clothes. Don't touch anything. Get in and stand under the water until I tell you to get out.'

'But—'

'Go,' he barked in such a tone that she fled without a word.

She stood under the water for fifteen minutes. Twenty minutes. Minutes while the world shifted.

She shook the entire time.

People came to check on her. Harry first, hauling open the bathroom door, staring in with fear, but his face sagging in relief as he saw she was alive, upright, not hurt.

'Lily?' she whispered.

'She's fine. We've got her out. Stay there,' he said. 'Charles says it's safest.' He left again.

So she stayed there. She couldn't think of anything else to do. She knew exactly why Charles had ordered her to do what she was doing. If there were fragments of broken shell on her clothes and she touched them…

She mustn't.

She stood, numbed and shocked, while the water streamed over her. She let her mind go blank. She couldn't imagine what was happening in the other room.

She didn't want to imagine.

Marcia came in then, white-faced, terrified.

'Are you OK?'

'I… Yes.'

'I can't stay,' she said, sounding apologetic. 'I need to—'

'I know.'

'Charles says keep your hands away from your sides. Don't attempt to get your clothes off. We'll do it with gloves as soon…'

She faltered.

'I'm OK,' Jill whispered.

Marcia gave her a scared glance and left.

There was noise coming from the other room. Appalling noise. She turned the water up and put her head under water, trying to block it out.

Dear God.

The noise subsided. The sound of horror gave way to the sound of subdued voices.

And finally he came. Charles. Pushing the door wide. Wheeling into the room.

Looking like death.

'Oh, Charles…'

'He's dead,' he said bluntly, and she cringed back against the tiles.

'Kelvin…'

'He never stood a chance,' he said. 'He went into cardiac arrest but with venom on his face there was no way we could give him mouth to mouth. Not without a mask. Even if—'

'Don't say it.'

'No,' he said, and looked at her. 'You're alive,' he said, as if he couldn't quite believe it. 'You know how long it took to get from the hospital to here?'

'You knew?'

'Harry had his photograph faxed through and left it on my desk. I'd seen him on the beach. God, help me, I'd accepted his offer to dispose of the shell. I hit the panic button for Harry but—'

'You got here first.'

'If he'd killed you, I think I would have died,' he said simply, and she stared out through the shower screen at the man she loved and felt her world shift all over again.

'Charles…'

'You want to come out?' he said, opening the screen door. 'I have gloves.'

'Gloves?'

'You think I'd let anyone else undress you?'

She smiled at that. It was a poor excuse for a smile but it was a smile for all that. She could hardly see him through tears.

'L-Lily?' she managed.

'Marcia's taken her over to the hospital. Would you believe she didn't even wake up? Our bedroom's a crime scene now, roped off for the coroner. I've done a fast change, I'm clean. But you were right there when it smashed. Marcia's brought you a robe. We'll go over to Mike and Emily's bungalow.'

'But—'

'All the stuff in the bedroom has to be cleaned before it's touched,' he said roughly. 'There's shards of shell everywhere. Come here.'

She stepped out onto the bathmat. He wouldn't let her help. Wearing heavy gardener's gloves and armed with a pair of scissors, he simply sliced her clothes off her.

He wrapped her in a towel, propelled her onto the bathroom stool and combed her hair. Over and over.

Then he had her put her head over the basin while he rinsed her hair so thoroughly that no trace of shell could remain.

'Stand up,' he said at last, and she did. He tugged the towel from her and held out another.

She went to take it from him, but he took her hands and he pulled her into him so she was cradled against him, cradled like a child, wrapped in a clean, dry towel, her hair still dripping, but safe.

Safe.

'I thought I'd lost you,' he whispered, and he held her close with something akin to wonder.

'It was the best throw,' she managed, still struggling to believe it was over.

'You realise we're going to have to get Ritz decontaminated?' He was striving from lightness but she could still hear the raw emotion in his voice.

'We could throw him out,' she said. 'Buy another one?'

'Are you kidding? He saved your life.'

'You saved my life,' she said, turning into him and hooking his face in her hands. 'You. My hero. My wonderful, sexy, fantastic Charles. My love.'

He stilled. 'You say that now…'

'How can I not say it?' she demanded. 'What did you tell Kelvin? That he had a whole body, he was capable of giving me the loving I deserved. Oh, Charles, as if you're not.'

'You're so beautiful,' he whispered, his face in her hair.

'I'm not beautiful. Once…'

'What the hell are you talking about?' he demanded, and put her away from him. 'Look at you. Look at you!' He turned her, swinging the chair so they were both staring into the bathroom mirror. She was curled on his knee. Before she could stop him he'd tugged the towel away so she was naked. She made a grab for the towel but he smiled and tossed it to the far side of the bathroom.

'No. Why cover it up?' He gazed into the mirror, soaking in every inch of her. 'What a waste, to cover it. You're every inch a woman, the most beautiful woman I know. From the moment I first saw you I wanted you.'

'You can't have done.'

'Don't tell me what I can and can't have done,' he said roughly, grasping her still tighter. 'Not while I'm holding you. Not while I have you. Not when I thought I'd lost you. But you're alive and wonderful and I have you in my arms and you're wearing my ring.'

'You wanted me?' she whispered, awed.

'For years,' he said simply. 'Only every time I approached you, you reacted like you didn't want to know me.'

'Oh, Charles,' she managed. 'I wanted you, too.'

'Excuse me?' he said in a strange voice, and she tugged back still further so she could see his face.

'I wanted you,' she said simply. 'The first time I met you I thought you were the most gorgeous doctor—the most fabulous man—I'd ever met. But you were rich and powerful and you could have any woman you wanted.'

'You're saying you wanted me?'

'I want you,' she said simply, still not believing. 'I love you, Charles. I love you with every inch of my being. Yes, I want a daughter. Yes, I agreed to marry you so we could adopt Lily. But I would have taken you on whatever terms I could get. I—'

'No,' he said, the awe in her voice echoed in his. 'My turn. I love you, Jill. I always thought…'

'Then stop thinking,' she said, half laughing, half crying. 'Let's both stop thinking. This is crazy. Oh, Charles, Kelvin's just died…'

'Do you mind?'

Her smile faded. 'I wouldn't have wanted him dead,' she said.

'But now he is, you're free to choose your life,' he said. 'Without fear. You're free to choose your own path.'

'I have,' she said simply. 'I choose you.'

'Jill…'

'Yes?'

'This is not going to work,' he said, goaded. 'Your clothes have contaminated the floor. There's a crime scene outside. I can't…'

'Yes, you can,' she said serenely. 'You can do anything you want, Charles Wetherby. Let's see a bit of that great improvisation you're famous for. I depend on you, my love. Starting now.'

* * *

It was the wedding to end all weddings. The chapel in Crocodile Creek was far too small to hold all the people who'd decided they wanted to attend. Jill and Charles had no control over their guest list.

'We've been waiting for this for eight long years,' Dora Grubb decreed. 'Do you think it's your wedding? It's our wedding.'

They came from all around the world. Doctors, nurses, paramedics who'd worked in Crocodile Creek and on Wallaby Island since the inception of the medical service. Patients Charles had cared for. Farming families who owed their ability to stay on the land to the medical service Charles had set up.

So many people…. The locals built a mini-chapel on the beach, an altar, an arch the bride had to walk through, paving set down specially so Charles could stand…

He stood, with Walter Grubb by his side. So many people to choose from for his best man… It had to be Grubby, caretaker of Crocodile Creek hospital.

Dora was matron of honour, gorgeous in purple taffeta, swelling fit to burst. Georgie had been asked but she'd pulled out at the last minute.

'Sorry, sweetie, even though I'm an obstetrician I have no control over what's happening to me at the moment. I'd have to carry a bucket instead of a bouquet.'

She was in the front row, wearing scarlet, looking pale but serenely happy with her Alistair. Alistair was carrying a bucket adorned with red bows.

Lily was flower girl. Of course. She wore a lacy confection of the palest pink with a huge pink satin bow at the back. She had silver and pink ribbons in her hair. There was no hint of tomboy Lily on this, the wedding day of her parents. She was determined to do this right.

As they all were. The crowd of friends clustered close, gasping their pleasure as Jill appeared.

She had no one to give her away.

'I'll be giving myself to you,' she told Charles with a hint of the austerity she'd been renowned for. 'As you'll be giving yourself to me.' And who could argue with that?

And she walked steadily down the beach toward her love. First came Dora, then Lily, scattering rose petals.

After her came four little boys, CJ, Danny, Robbie and Sam. They were there to hold her train. They were also there to celebrate the end of a nightmare and the moving forward into a future full of hope.

Six attendants. One labradoodle, tailing wagging furiously, bringing up the rear.

One bride.

Charles had eyes only for his bride.

His Jill.

She'd dressed simply. Her ivory silk gown had a low-cut bodice and tiny capped sleeves. The dress fitted perfectly to her waist, then flared out to lovely sweeping folds of soft silk, shimmering around her.

He'd never seen anything more beautiful in his life.

Where was the prickly, defensive woman of the past bleak years now? In the last four weeks she'd blossomed, flowered. She smiled at him mistily through tears, and it was as much as Charles could do not to weep himself.

This woman… His Jill…

He stood before her. Her Charles. He'd abandoned his wheelchair and his crutches for the day. There was a slim handrail near the makeshift altar and it was enough. Planning for later, when they'd walk out through the throng of well-wishers as man and wife, he'd said simply, 'I'll lean on you.'

And she'd lean on him, she thought. For ever.

Her Charles. Impossibly handsome in his black dinner suit. Impossibly wonderful. Impossible to believe he'd be her husband.

She reached him. He took her hand and held it.

He smiled into her eyes, and his smile was declaration enough before any vows could be spoken.

Man and wife. From this day forth.

And then there was the wedding gift from the town. Organised by Harry.

They hadn't wanted to go far away tonight, for there were so many friends from overseas that they intended this party to end all parties to go on for all the weekend. But as their wedding day faded toward dusk they disappeared, promising their guests they'd see them tomorrow but tonight they had things to do, places to go…

Their guests all knew where they were going. Even Lily had serenely granted them leave of absence to get this honeymoon over with. For it was planned. The carpenters were busy knocking walls out of their apartments. The town had therefore arranged alternative accommodation.

A tiny cove, just north of the town. A secluded beach. One of the loveliest places in the world.

Their friends had been at work and as Charles and Jill arrived, knowing only they'd been ordered to come here, not knowing what to expect, they gasped in wonder.

A marquee had been erected just past the high-tide mark. It was a beribboned confection of a honeymoon palace.

They made their way down the beach in wonder.

The marquee was set up as a honeymoon suite. Inside were rich silk rugs covering the sand. There was a vast, king-sized bed festooned with silk hangings, pillows and quilts, like something out of an Eastern harem.

There was a portable bathroom to the side. With a full-sized bath! A tank of fresh water was connected through the wall.

There was a refrigerator brimming with a feast fit for royalty.

The flaps on the far side of the marquee were open to the sea, the high-tide mark right there. The moonlit beach beckoned.

There was a notice attached to the tent wall.

'Welcome to your honeymoon. The cove's been searched and netted so thoroughly not even a tadpole can get through. The access road was cordoned off by the police the minute you went through, and security's in place. Nobody, nothing gets into this cove for however long you want it. With love. CC.'

Crocodile Creek. Their friends. Their family.

'It's perfect,' Charles said.

'You're perfect,' Jill whispered.

'Maybe not,' he admitted, cautious still. 'Do you remember what you said back at Wallaby Island? That we'll never get to know our wobbly bits while the lights are out? I guess this is the perfect time to examine our wobbly bits.'

'So it's time for an anatomy lesson,' she said softly.

'I'm thinking it might be.' He smiled at her, that heart-melting smile she loved so much. 'It seems a shame to take off that beautiful dress.'

'It seems a shame to take off that gorgeous suit.'

He nodded. His eyes darkened with laughter and with something else.

'I'm ready when you are,' he said.

'Right,' she said, and grinned and threw reserve and caution and everything else she could think of to the wind.

Celebrate 100 years of pure reading pleasure with Mills & Boon®

To mark our centenary, each month we're publishing a special 100th Birthday Edition. These celebratory editions are packed with extra features and include a FREE bonus story.

Plus, you have the chance to enter a fabulous monthly prize draw. See 100th Birthday Edition books for details.

Now that's worth celebrating!

September 2008
Crazy about her Spanish Boss by Rebecca Winters
Includes FREE bonus story
Rafael's Convenient Proposal

November 2008
**The Rancher's Christmas Baby
by Cathy Gillen Thacker**
Includes FREE bonus story *Baby's First Christmas*

December 2008
One Magical Christmas by Carol Marinelli
Includes FREE bonus story *Emergency at Bayside*

Look for Mills & Boon® 100th Birthday Editions at your favourite bookseller or visit
www.millsandboon.co.uk

FREE!

4 Books
and a surprise gift!

We would like to take this opportunity to thank you for reading this Mills & Boon® book by offering you the chance to take FOUR more specially selected titles from the Medical™ series absolutely FREE! We're also making this offer to introduce you to the benefits of the Mills & Boon® Book Club™—

- ★ **FREE home delivery**
- ★ **FREE gifts and competitions**
- ★ **FREE monthly Newsletter**
- ★ **Exclusive Mills & Boon Book Club offers**
- ★ **Books available before they're in the shops**

Accepting these FREE books and gift places you under no obligation to buy, you may cancel at any time, even after receiving your free shipment. Simply complete your details below and return the entire page to the address below. You don't even need a stamp!

YES! Please send me 4 free Medical books and a surprise gift. I understand that unless you hear from me, I will receive 6 superb new titles every month for just £2.99 each, postage and packing free. I am under no obligation to purchase any books and may cancel my subscription at any time. The free books and gift will be mine to keep in any case.

M8ZEF

Ms/Mrs/Miss/Mr ....Initials ....

Surname ....

Address ....**BLOCK CAPITALS PLEASE**

....

....Postcode ....

Send this whole page to:
UK: FREEPOST CN81, Croydon, CR9 3WZ